D1240564

MILDRED'S GARDEN

laura boggess

the poetry club series

ts T. S. Poetry Press • New York

T. S. Poetry Press
Briarcliff, New York
Tspoetry.com
© 2021 by Laura Boggess

Cover image by Nathalie Stickelbaut
www.nathalie-photos.com

ISBN 978-1-943120-52-9

Cataloging-in-Publication Data:
Boggess, Laura
    [Fiction.]
    Mildred's Garden.
      The poetry club series/Laura Boggess
    ISBN 978-1-943120-52-9

thank you, lan and azzat—
you and your families make our world
a more beautiful place

SAM

[june-july]

Mildred kept a garden.

And apparently a pretty serious one.

Sam leaned back into his deck chair on this sultry night and used his left thumb to deftly scroll through her Instagram feed.

Mildred, face half hidden by a honey-colored sunflower. Mildred, long-stemmed blossoms over her shoulder—walking away. Peeking from behind a huge golden flower. What in the world was it? He squinted in the dim light: Dahlia. Never heard of it. There she was, face buried in Chinese tangerine roses. Another with a daisy behind her ear. Rubbing noses with a tiny hound puppy, some kind of lacy white blooms crowning her hair. A puppy! He scrolled through photo after photo of bright florals and vegetables: tomatoes, snap peas, radishes, pole beans. Mingled throughout were glimpses of Mildred. Mildred with her moon-face and that luminous smile.

He kept scrolling until he arrived at the picture of them. The one time they'd met. It was at the Mountain Stage show in January. She and her friend Cindy were lingering at the merch table. Usually he didn't mingle with the fans, preferring to slip away after finishing his set. But Mountain Stage was always different. It was his third time on the show and it felt like a homecoming. The Stage had a kind of family feeling—an artist's village. Everyone celebrating everyone else. Making music and life.

It was good. And so he was feeling safe. He wandered out to the front while a bluegrass trio was doing their thing on stage. What was the name of that band? He couldn't remember. They were talented—all about the three-part harmony. Cute lead vocal. But he was feeling like one more banjo and fiddle number would do him in. So he slipped out.

When Mildred saw him she froze, a vinyl copy of *Another Time Around the Sun* in her hands. Behind her, Cindy held up a T-shirt with the *Oddbird* album cover art on it. At Mildred's sudden paralysis, she, too, looked up and in his direction.

"Oh, my gosh!" She tossed the shirt and tugged Mildred toward him.

He took off his hat and inclined his head at their approach. "Hello, ladies." Cindy did all the talking. Mildred beamed.

We're your number one fans. Well, Mildred has always been you're your number one fan. She's followed you since Paper Lanterns, how long has that been anyway? She has all your stuff, even when you were with The Robber Barons. We love Oddbird! *Mildred says it's a little more contemplative than your others...*

On and on Cindy chatted, while he—amused—nodded and smiled, until he looked up and was caught by Mildred's almond eyes. Finally, Mildred—never breaking his gaze—pressed a hand on Cindy's forearm. Then she reached out to him, slender ivory fingers extended. When she opened her mouth, all he heard was something like birdsong—a lilting melody that made his heart hurt. He took her hand and lifted her fingers to his lips, struggling to hear words in her voice but failing. Her skin smelled like apples, sweet in the sun. At the slight pressure of his lips, she blushed and dipped her head to the side—dark hair falling like rain across her shoulder. She smiled and a dimple appeared in her left cheek, making his breath catch. He blinked into the song of her voice. He felt like he was being sirened.

But he was bound to the mast of the ship of the show and when Paul, the stage manager, hailed him, the spell was broken.

"Gil! Time to warm up. You're on deck."

"All right, man, I'll be right there."

The women quickly snapped a couple photos with him and he returned backstage to get ready for his set, softly cradling against his chest the hand she'd held—reluctant to let go of the feel of her skin.

Later, Mildred tagged him in this shot: she, dimpling into the frame and he gazing down where her fingers encircled his. He liked the picture and impulsively followed her stream. When she requested to follow him back, he hesitated.

His Instagram feed was private. Facebook was for his fans but Instagram was the place he reserved for those who knew more of him than his music. It was the place he kept up with his nieces' lives—gawked at Abby's pictures of Peter the Oversized Rabbit and Della's ballet poses. It was the one place his little sister Sher knew she could say what needed saying. Like, "It's time to come home." Or, "When was the last time anyone grilled you a steak as big as your plate?"

He didn't post often, only when he wanted to share *something specific* with *someone specific*. There was the string of ex-girlfriends, and his posse from high school; his philosophy professor from the one year at University…and Heather. Of course, Heather. He'd only had to block a couple people he'd let in. Instagram was private. The place of the inside joke and the tired out reference.

But he accepted Mildred's follow request.

Sam studied the picture, noting every detail already memorized. They could be brother and sister—dark hair, just a hint of the Far East around the eyes. For the millionth time he wondered about her story. She was obviously of mixed heritage, like him. Was she adopted too? Or did she grow up in the culture that gave her such disquieting beauty? As with his, there were no clues in her feed about her background.

He scrolled back up. Mildred's pictures left him with a gaping hole somewhere inside. No, that wasn't fair. The hole was already there. Her pictures only made him more aware of it.

Just then, a new post popped up in her feed. It was a black and white photo of Mildred standing barefoot in a sea of red poppies. The poppies were the only color in the image. Mildred was holding a plain poster-board with a large black question mark on it. Her head tipped downward to read the sign along with him. The accompanying comment said, "Big announcement coming soon!"

Sam breathed deep of the night air and studied the fast-appearing comments.

sologirl Is it what I think it is???

gregthebear About time!

taniaflorist Can't wait!

mom2four Yay!

He thumbed a quick one. "**@mildredsgarden** Moonflower, what are u up to?"

Mildred rarely replied to her comments, but she almost always answered his. "**@giltheguitarman** you'll just have to wait and see ;)"

~

Sam's phone vibrated on the bedside table. He opened his eyes and stretched his arms above his head. The sun burned through the flimsy curtains, exposing the room-air for what it was: all stale, silver bits of floating dust. The phone stilled. But he knew she'd call right back. He rolled over and picked it up just as it started again.

"Yeah." There was no use avoiding.

"Great show the other night." Her smoky voice tickled his ear.

"Thanks, Babe. I'm glad you came."

"But where did you go after? I lost you and then you were just…gone."

"I was tired, Heather. I've done five shows this week. This tour is a killer. All I want to do on these two weeks off is sleep."

There was silence on the other end. Then: "I just missed you, that's all."

He took a long breath in. Closed his eyes and he was a kid again, wearing that ratty baseball cap his dad had given him. And he was mad. He couldn't hit the ball the way he wanted. Whenever he lined up, he swung the bat with all his might, but it never struck true. Always too high or too low—in the wrong place to make a ball fly. He threw down the bat. "I quit! I hate this stupid game!" He stalked off and plopped down in the dugout. In his mind he waited. This was his favorite part. His dad's image was so clear. He remembered every detail of Thom Gillenwater's face that day: the five o'clock shadow, the way his brow crinkled, that one out-of-control cowlick swooping back from his forehead…

His dad sat beside him. "Shh," he said, leaning in and holding his index finger over his lips. When he had Sam's attention he would ask, "Do you hear that, Sammy?" He fell for it every time. "Hear what, Dad?" Thom would lean in even closer and whisper, "Your heart, son. If you breathe real slow and quiet you can hear it better. Listen."

Sam listened now. He'd been practicing listening to his heart all of his life—until the listening was a part of him. Right now, just the memory of his dad left his heart in a slow, steady thrum. He imagined love like a golden balloon lifting him into the sky. It never took long.

"Gil? Why did you leave without me the other night?"

He came back to the dust-filled light.

"Seemed like you had other things going on."

"What are you talking about, Gillenwater? Just because I was looking for Joe doesn't mean what you think. He had something for me. I just needed to pick it up, that's all."

"I thought as much."

"Gil! I wasn't taking anything! I swear."

"You know how I feel about that guy. About that stuff. I don't want any part of it."

"I know, Babe, but you've been on the road for three months now. A girl's gotta pass the time somehow. I'm all done now. I swear. And I really want to see you. I need to see you."

Sam sighed. "It doesn't work like that."

"I'm on my way over. I'll make you a good lunch. You've probably been eating nothing but crap. I'll stop at the market and pick up some fresh eggs and spinach. We'll have a frittata. I saw some beautiful heirlooms the other day. They would be perfect."

His stomach growled as she talked on about red onions and feta cheese. Who was he kidding? When she started talking food, he always gave in. She was his best friend. And the sex was good. He just couldn't trust a damn thing that came out of her mouth anymore.

"Or maybe goat cheese? Would you rather goat cheese?"

"All right, all right. Give me time to get cleaned up." He hated himself as he said it. "You know I can't stand goat cheese."

After she hung up he couldn't move. This endless loop, this constant repeat—when would he quit this thing? He swung his legs over the bed and collected the elastic band off the table, pulled his thick hair back into a short ponytail. Then he crouched down to look under the bed.

The orange crate was still there, same as always, same as the first day he moved into this place. Maybe the only relic left of his childhood, it had followed him from his parents' house, to the failed attempt at college, the six months in New York and then here, Nashville.

He slid it out and rummaged around the bottom. It had to be here somewhere. He'd stashed a pack before Christmas. He hadn't smoked since January, but just the thought of Heather—here at his house—set off an alarm of craving in his entire body. *There!*

He pulled the pack out from under some long-abandoned song lyrics, tapped it firm against the palm of his hand and pulled out a single. He stuffed the rest back under the papers and slid the crate into its hidey hole. He found some matches in the bedside table drawer and walked out onto the balcony, phone in hand. Leiper's Fork wasn't too close or too far from downtown—tucked away in a sweet piece of woods his builders carefully pruned to stay wild, but not too wild. He loved this little cabin. The country rolled right up to his back door, but he was still convenient to the recording studio and the clubs he played on weeknights.

The Nashville noise felt far away as he leaned on the railing and breathed in the quick-disappearing dew of late morning.

A doe teetered at the tree line, white tail flicking nervously. She edged forward cautiously and two spotted fawns emerged behind her. She approached the salt-lick he had put out last year and soon her tail stopped worrying. One of her babies kicked up its heels and frolicked across the back lawn. Something stirred inside him and Mildred's face came to mind.

He'd almost forgotten: her big announcement! He dropped down in his watching chair and tapped up her feed.

Welcome to The Gardens: Bed and Breakfast and Retreat Center.

It was a series of shots, a story in images. A picture of Mildred and Cindy, arms across each other's shoulders, heads leaned together, both with happy smiles.

We've been dreaming and working for two years and finally, our dream is coming true!

A rustic farmhouse, a large pondish-like lake, flowers, flowers, and more flowers.

If you want the details, read our interview in this morning's Sunday Gazette. Link in profile.

He scrolled up to the profile and clicked over.

"Local Activist Settles Down."

Was Mildred an "activist?"

He skimmed through the article. It was Mildred's family farm, left to her when her mother passed away three years ago. Mildred's mother loved flowers and had cultivated five acres surrounding the farmhouse with both native and rare varieties of blooms designed for color in every season.

"When my mother left her birth country of Vietnam as a young bride and made the United States her home, the only thing she brought with her was a love for all growing things," Mildred said. "Well, that, and her cousin, who I called uncle, *Van Minh.*

Over a lifetime—together—they created these gardens of the four *qui,* or the four seasons, so they would always have a little piece of their homeland with them."

Mildred's mother was Vietnamese. Sam let that sink in, feeling as if the bottom had dropped out of his world. He scrolled back to her Instagram feed.

"**@mildredsgarden** Congrats on your new venture, Moon-flower. Next #mountainstage, save me a room."

He thought to say something about her mother but didn't know what. So he hit "share" and sat with the pictures of Mildred's beautiful world for a minute.

The response was almost immediate.

"**@giltheguitarman** you have an open invitation. Any. Time. I'll fluff the pillows even."

This made him smile. And blush a little. But before he could respond, the phone started to buzz in his hand, his sister's name blacking out the images of Mildred's new endeavor.

"Hey, sister, what's up?"

"Hello, brother, I miss you."

"I miss you more."

"I'm serious, Sam Gillenwater. I don't want to wait until Thanksgiving to see you. Will you come and do a house concert for us? I have skills. I can do a GoFundMe to pay for it. We could even give part of it to your favorite charity. After I pay for your ticket and your time, that is. I'm sure it's not a conflict of interest."

Sam laughed.

"It sounds like the beginnings of a brilliant plan. I haven't seen the girls in six months. I bet they won't even recognize me."

"I know, right? What is that stuff on your chin I saw on the Facebook post from last night? You know the girls hate facial hair. It scares them."

He laughed. "Tell the girls not to worry. I couldn't grow a full beard if I tried. Laziness is all this is." He cupped his stubbly chin in his hand and ran his fingers through the bare beginnings.

A knock at the door. *Damn. He hadn't even gotten a shower.*

"Let me think about it, Sher. There's that show in Boston. It's only an hour or so from you. I'll look at the schedule. But I have to call you back. Heather's at the door."

"Heather? Are you still messing around with her?"

"Careful, now. You know she's a good friend. She's my best friend."

"*You* be careful. Have you forgotten what happened over Christmas? Besides, I thought *I* was your best friend."

"You're my sister. That doesn't count."

There was bustling in the kitchen, the rustle of grocery bags. Heather still had her key.

"Look, I gotta go. I'll call you tomorrow, and we'll figure something out."

"Promise?"

"Promise."

"Okay. I love you, big brother."

"Love you more."

He hung up and went back inside, stashing the unsmoked cigarette in the side table drawer before heading into the kitchen. Heather was dicing onions. She looked up when he walked in, pointed at him with the knife.

"You look like hell."

"I know, I'm sorry. Sher caught me on the phone and I haven't even gotten a shower yet."

"Sher, huh?" She eyed him dubiously, then shrugged

offhandedly. "Well, I guess she's still your sister." She picked up the onion and resumed chopping. "Why don't you go ahead and shower while I make lunch?" she said, glancing up and over him. The brown skin under her eyes was rimmed in purple and she looked like she'd lost weight. Her usually tame, tightly kinked hair was a frizzy halo around her head. It was always awkward between them when he'd been on the road for a while. He stood in the doorway, arms overhead, fingers gripping the top of the door frame. He shifted from foot to foot, conscious of his bare chest. She was too, he could tell, and he saw her eyes move down the length of his body. A too-short lock of hair slipped the band and fell into his eyes.

"Okay," he said, finally. But he didn't move until she put the knife down, held his eyes with hers, moved slow toward him, smoothed back that wayward lock of hair with her fingers, pressed herself against him until they were one.

~

In the night, he felt her body warm against him and pulled her closer. He slept better than he had for months.

~

He awakened to the smell of bacon and he smiled. Something about her stirrings in the kitchen slowed his heart rate and evened out his breathing. He listened. She mused a song as she worked, and he recognized the title track to *Oddbird*.

Oddbird, she said, why don't you
fly away, fly away, let
the ripening of August

steal your song;
the world is made of dew
and I am a blade of grass—
tremble
tremble
beneath your stare, it goes
through me
like the sun
shines through
clear glass
Oddbird, she said...

Her voice dropped and she made a little choking sound. He felt her standing still in the kitchen. Then he heard her feet pad away.

He let out a long, slow breath and rubbed his eyes with his fingers.

It was music that had brought them together. When they met, she was working as a studio vocalist. She did some backing vocals on his first album. That was almost sixteen years ago. They were just kids. He remembered how excited she was to sing with him. She had met him at the door of the studio that first time nearly bouncing out of her skin.

"Your songs are amazing! I can't wait to get these tracks down!"

Sweet, that's what she was. She was all goodness and big heart. He was just starting then, so her excitement meant a lot. He had a little buzz from a couple competitions he'd won regionally. Two of his songs had been picked up by some big names. He'd been in town for a year before the break came.

He didn't know many people except a few musicians he'd played with around town. When she met Sam at that studio door it opened doors inside *him*. For the first time, *he believed*. He believed he could make it.

Heather grew up in Connecticut but came to Nashville to go to school. She was working on a B.A. in voice from Vanderbilt when their paths crossed. She'd been singing in clubs— mostly covers. But she was starting to write too. Her voice was like no one's he'd ever heard. A cross between Allison Krauss and Macy Gray. Bluegrass soul, that's what she was. And when she would sing with him, she made him better. She was dating a guy she'd been with all through high school who was finishing up his second year of med school. She really loved that dickhead, who knew nothing about music. The guy was always studying, or working, or had some other reason not to be with Heather. So she and Sam ended up hanging out most days. Heather showed him the best of Nashville—all the cool local spots the students knew. And she cheered him on with his songwriting— sang with him, played the keys when he needed her to. She even went on a few gigs with him when he wanted more vocals. They told each other everything.

Two years later, the boyfriend had left her for another resident and Heather was sharing Sam's bed. He stared at the ceiling and listened inside himself. A wave of something big and heavy rolled over him and he closed his eyes and let the truth become still water: he missed the way they were back then. He missed the simplicity of their friendship. He didn't want to cross that line, even then. He knew better. But her heart was broken and he was lonely too. They'd been on and off ever since. He knew he loved Heather, but he also knew it wasn't the kind of love it takes to make a life together. They stayed with it because they didn't know what else to do.

Heather wasn't singing anymore, which broke his heart. She'd lost the drive. Scrubbing clubs every night wore her down. She'd taken a more reliable job, teaching voice and piano at Belmont University, a small liberal arts college in town. It was just how things worked out. Only she was miserable teaching. The smoking and the drugs…they weren't a part of the Heather he knew back then.

Remembering, he must have dozed off because when the smoke alarm sounded, he startled awake. The bacon was burning. Sam jumped out of bed and ran in the kitchen. No Heather. But the pan was smoking like crazy. He turned the fire off and lifted it from the stove, reached up and pulled the battery from the alarm.

A familiar fear licked his insides. "Heather?" No Heather in the living room. He opened a window as he continued looking, trying to clear the smoky air. The bathroom door off the entry was closed and locked. He knocked loudly, leaning his forehead against the door.

"Heather? You okay?" He shouldered the door but it wouldn't budge. *Think, Sam, think!* He ran out to the garage and frantically rummaged through his toolbox. He found a thin nail and ran back inside, threaded it through the narrow hole on the doorknob and pressed gently until he felt the lock release. She was on the floor up against the door.

"Heather!" He pushed in, shoving her body with the door so he could squeeze by. He checked her pulse. It was slow. So very slow. He smoothed her hair out of her face, bent closer and listened to her breath. Her eyes were open but she wasn't there.

The skin around her mouth was a blueish-gray, purple in spots. He shook her roughly. "Heather! Wake up! Oh, God, oh God, oh God..."

He ran back in the bedroom and grabbed his phone, dialing 9-1-1 as he ran back to Heather. "Hello? Yes, I have an emergency! An overdose, I think. 52 Moonrise Drive. Leiper's. What? I don't know, I..." He spun around, took in the leather strap trailing loose around her forearm, saw the needle on the floor beside her, spoon and lighter on the sink. "Heroin, I think. Yes, she's still breathing. Please hurry! Oh, God, she's vomiting."

The operator talked him through what to do until he heard the sirens. It all seemed to be happening in slow motion. He opened the door for the gurney, the black and white uniforms, the oxygen mask, the injection in her thigh. A buzzing sound in his head. They wouldn't let him ride in the ambulance. He stood in the driveway in his boxers, shaking, watching flashing lights move farther and farther away.

~

She'd been asleep for 12 hours. The doctor said that happened sometimes, not to worry, she was very lucky. They got the Narcan in her on time. He waited by her bed, holding her hand, singing her favorite songs in a quiet voice. She just kept sleeping. He tried to call her parents, but the answering machine kicked on over and over. He did not have Janet's cell number.

A lab technician came in to draw Heather's blood. "I can step out a minute," he said.

"There's no need," her smile was all sunshine. "I'm just drawing a little blood. No big deal."

"It's a big deal to me. Fainter, every time."

"Oh, you're one of *those*." Just look away, honey. This will only take a minute."

He needed a reason to leave. A cup of coffee would help.

Sam put his hand over Heather's. So cold. He pulled the blanket up close around her chin and rubbed her cinnamon cheek. "Don't go anywhere," he said. "I'll be right back."

He was still looking at her when he slipped through the door. That's why he didn't see them.

"There he is!" He turned around to a camera in his face. Flashes fired from every direction. "Please don't..." He lifted up his hand to fend them off.

"Gil! Gil—over here! Mr. Gillenwater, I understand your long-term girlfriend Heather Watts is in that room. Can you tell us what happened?" She stuck a mic in his face as a cameraman zoomed in. Others were behind them, shouting questions. "Was it a drug overdose, Gil?" A man in the back. "This isn't the first time, is it? Is she going to be okay?" A woman in a red jacket. "Will you talk to us about heroin, Gil?" "Were you with her when it happened?"

Sam blinked into the assault, emotion and fatigue making him dull. One of the nurses came to his aid. "You all can't be here." She held up both hands as if to push them along. "You're disturbing our patients and their families. Please respect these people's privacy."

Three security guards appeared and the reporters started to disperse, still shouting questions.

"Gil! If you want to talk, call Connie at *The Register*." "Gil, just one statement!" The guards pushed them along down the hall and Sam, stunned, slipped back into Heather's room.

The nurse came in behind him. "I'm so sorry. I don't know

how that happened. They were sitting in the waiting area, pretending to be someone's family. Someone on staff must have leaked that you were here."

"I just wanted a cup of coffee."

"Now *that,* I can do." She went out and returned with the coffee, as well as a sheet and blanket for the reclining chair. He scooted the chair as close as he could to the bed so he could check on Heather periodically. He was tucking the sheet in around the cushions when she opened her eyes.

"Do you remember the first day we met?"

He spun around. "Babe? Heather!"

His voice broke with her name and his knees buckled. He took her face in his hands and pressed his forehead to hers. "You nearly scared me to death," he said, tears coming.

"I know." Her voice was a whisper. "I'm sorry."

"Babe, what were you thinking? When did you start with that stuff? If I'd known I would've killed Joe. I might still kick his ass if I ever see him again. You could have died." He smoothed loose strands of hair away from her face, running his hands over and over her unruly curls with no effect.

She lifted her eyes to his. Hers were red and puffy, her skin drained.

"Do you remember the day we met?"

"Of course I do. How could I ever forget it? It was at the studio on 29th."

"Do you remember what you told me? That first day? After we sang together?"

Sam searched his mind, heart still pounding. "I don't remember the exact words, but I know it was good. You were the best singer I'd ever worked with."

Heather smiled a tremulous smile. "That's what you said. That I was the best you'd ever heard."

"You were."

Tears streamed down her face. "And you said we made a good team. You and me. A good team."

Sam stopped messing with her hair and let his hand slide down to cup her cheek. "We did," he said. "We do."

"We *did*," she said, eyes glistening, "but not anymore. I miss *you*, Gil. I miss *me*."

Sam's shoulders caved, but he didn't break her gaze.

"Let's not talk about this now. First, we need to get you well. You can stay at the cabin. I'll call around. Find the best treatment center that's not too far off…"

She looked away. "I want to go home, Gil."

"Home?"

"Yes. Back to Connecticut."

Sam sat down.

"Mom's been trying to get me to come home for a while. She wants me to go into treatment up there. I've still got two months before the semester starts back up. Enough time to decide if I—if I can do this. I don't want to lose my job but," her voice broke, "I don't want to—I don't want to live like this anymore."

Sam took her hands. "Whatever you need. I've got two weeks before the tour starts back up. I'll go with you, get you settled…"

"No!"

She said it so emphatically, he dropped her hands and sat back down, looked at the floor.

"Look," her voice gentler now. "Whatever this is between us, it isn't working. You've known it a lot longer than I, Gil.

We were great as friends, but as lovers..."

Her breath caught. "We're. It's been. A slow drowning. We need to let go. We can do *that* for each other, at least."

He knew she was right. Hadn't he been fighting with himself over this very thing? Sam said nothing, just took her hand and kissed her fingers. They drifted into a comfortable silence and Heather fell back to sleep.

~

The med team wanted to keep her a couple more nights. Sam slept folded up in the recliner at her side. When the doctor released her, Sam took her back to her place for a few days until she started to bounce back. When she was ready, he helped her pack, drove her to the airport, and put her on a plane to Connecticut.

And when she cried into his neck before entering the security gate, he wanted to say it was his fault, that he would change, that everything would be okay. Then Mildred's face flashed in his mind.

And just like that, Heather was gone.

~

It wasn't until three weeks later that he discovered she'd left with a page from his poetry journal. It was neatly stolen: carefully torn along the binding so as not to be detected. For the life of him, he couldn't recall the missing words. Or think why she would have taken them without asking. A smattering of verse. A rhyme? A memory. A bare thread of what he owed her.

on a bed
of wild violets, on the edge

of a forest, on the edge
of a dusty road—your bare legs
in the cool of the morning

on our way to a Mississippi show
the greening of spring growing
greener with each mile,
your amber eyes dancing
with the music inside, you
dipped your sweet, brown fingers
into heart-shaped leaves,

"Did you know," you said,
"that you can eat these?" and
placed a single violet on my tongue,
the lace on the hem
of your peasant skirt
softly touching my fingers—

this is how
I remember you.

~

It was the loneliest few weeks. Sam was tortured by all the ways he may have contributed to the overdose. He wrote two songs in three hours. He ate nothing at all. Or he ate pizza. He power-watched the first five seasons of *Game of Thrones*.

He was almost out of tears when Mildred's private message came through.

mildredsgarden "Gil? Didn't know if I should say anything. Just found out about your friend Heather. Hope she's okay. Wanted to say I'm sorry."

He wondered briefly if it was weird that a woman he'd met only once and that he had a strange obsession with was trying to comfort him about his ex-girlfriend's drug overdose.

Maybe? But for some reason he found it sweet. A little awkward. But sweet.

giltheguitarman "Thanks. Been a rough few weeks. Heather's doing okay. She's with her family in Connecticut."

Should he tell Mildred he and Heather were not together? He thought about it for a second but decided to keep it simple. But Mildred wasn't done.

mildredsgarden "I'm sorry. Don't mean to be nosy. Just feeling sad for you and wanted you to know. I enjoy our friendship in this space, but it's strange how I can see images from your life every day and not really know what's going on in your world. This is just me saying I care about the other stuff too. If you ever need to talk, I'm a good listener."

These words made his eyes smart. It had been a while since anyone had offered to share his burdens. He knew Sher was always there, but it was hard to talk about Heather with his sister. They didn't exactly hit it off.

giltheguitarman "Thank you, Moonflower. Means a lot. Been feeling all the feelings. Heather and I've dated on & off over the years & recently decided we're better as friends. Been needing to happen for a while. Just wish I knew she needed help before finding out like this. Can't help feeling I failed her somehow."

mildredsgarden "I obviously don't know all the circumstances, but I know addicts are very good at hiding things. Many things. Don't be so hard on yourself. Sounds like you've been a good friend."

giltheguitarman "Thanks for saying that. Need to sit with this for a while. And thanks for the offer to listen. This back & forth has helped more than you know. Your pictures too. Keep sharing your garden. All that healing beauty. Hope the plans for the bed & breakfast are going well. Mildred? Please call me Sam. That's what my closest peeps call me."

They made a few other small-talk statements, but he was tired so he said goodnight. Besides, whatever this thing was with Mildred, he wasn't sure direct messaging on Instagram was the best way to figure it out.

That night he dreamed he was sleeping with his head in Mildred's lap. When he awakened he could still feel the featherlight touch of her fingers trailing through his hair.

~

She was holding a baby robin in cupped hands. "I've heard a tiny whisper in my heart," Mildred's new post said, "to care for those who need a fresh start. Do you want to help? Follow the link in my profile."

Sam scrolled to her profile and clicked the link.

It took him to a peaceful website for the new bed and breakfast. At the top was the picture from Instagram—Mildred holding a tiny chicklet. Beside it was a video blog titled "Begin Again."

He clicked *play* and tapped the full-screen mode arrows. Mildred's luminescent moon-face was looking back at him, her warm brown eyes alight. She reached back from the camera and settled into a high-backed wrought iron chair. There were trees behind her and the soft chirrup of insects filled the silence.

Mildred considered the camera and smiled. The way her lips moved made him lightheaded. He was floating.

"Hi, friends. I'm Mildred Ruffner, co-owner and operator of The Gardens, a bed and breakfast and events venue just outside of Charleston, West Virginia." Why did her voice make his heart race?

Sam hit *pause*. He shook his head and closed his eyes for a second. He wanted to savor the song in her voice—memorize the lilt and intonation. He swallowed and opened his eyes again, studied the stilled image on the screen. Something wild stirred inside him. He drew a breath and tapped *play* again and once more the earth seemed to drift beneath him.

"I'm sitting in one of my favorite spots on the property." She was wearing a white linen summer dress, loose-fitting and sleeveless. He traced the curve of her upper arm with his eyes. "Behind me you can see a part of our little Lake Anya, built by my father and named for my mother, who loved this land as much with her hands as she did with her heart." She paused and studied the lake. Her short nails were painted robin's egg blue. "Across the lake on this side, you can just barely see part of The Glasshouse, which provides a home to mother's expansive orchid collection and other more fragile flowers."

Sunlight played over her hair and she turned her face toward the light, closing her eyes, ever so briefly. She reminded him of a flower, opening to the sun. And then, Sam was in the blue. Soaring above Mildred. He looked down at the top of her head, felt the sun warm his back and shoulders. He could hear her voice and struggled to listen. He wanted to hear the words.

"I wanted to show you a little bit of this place, to say to you what a gift it was to grow up here. Not because of the beauty and comfort that was certainly a part of my life, but because it was *home*. A place I will always feel safe and loved."

She bowed her head and that hair—a silent waterfall—followed suit. She spoke without looking up.

"Several weeks ago I was invited to hear a guest speaker. Zahura Rasho was young and beautiful, and she shared a story through a translator—so tragic, so heartrending, that my eyes fill with tears as I remember the telling."

Mildred looked back up to the camera, eyes rimmed with tears. The flying sensation faded. Sam felt his feet solid on the earth.

"Zahura is one of the Yezidi people. When she was 16, she was taken prisoner along with thousands of other women and held as a sex slave. She was beaten and burned, humiliated and abused in countless ways. She managed to escape, through help from people who secretly found a way to free her and a handful of other captives. Since that time, she's been a voice for refugees everywhere.

Zahura's five brothers and her mother were murdered in the massacre of her village. Thousands were forced to flee, to leave their homes and all that was dear to them. They still wander—homeless and in need, fearful for their lives, trapped in internment camps, stripped of everything.

Many of these displaced families are seeking help from international communities. They seek a home where they will have a future and be safe. When I heard Zahura speak, I knew I had to help. Somehow."

Sam watched Mildred's fervid face shimmer.

"Hospitality has always been my gift. All my life I've grown things. I've made the earth hospitable to many things. When I was a girl, I helped mother grow her flowers all over this farm. In high school, I worked at Gritt's Greenhouse: learning, learning, learning. Always learning. Later, I opened the flower shop on Capital Street. Now my gardens serve a farm-to-table café in the bed and breakfast." She looked straight into the camera. "Now I want to swing my doors open wide to people who need a safe and beautiful place to make a fresh start."

She paused and dabbed at her eyes, shifting in her seat.

"One month from today, The Gardens will welcome a Yezidi family to West Virginia. The family we're hosting has two young daughters. Vian is eight, Lelia is twelve." Mildred leaned closer. Sam touched the curve of her face on his phone. Her eyes were endlessly deep. "Two girls we can give a chance to *begin again*."

Her face crumpled and she covered her eyes with both hands. "I'm sorry," she whispered through her fingers.

"We have a home waiting for this family, but it's still in need of many things. That's why I'm sharing this story with you. We'll be accepting donations at the greenhouse for the next two weeks. If you have any beautiful houseware items or furniture you'd like to give toward our cause, it would be so welcome. Monetary donations would also be welcome. You can find all the details you need on our website."

She smiled—a moonbeam. *Moonflower.*

"I know some of you will have questions. Please feel free to message me or call me any time, if you can't find what you need on the website. I love talking with my neighbors. And, thank you." She lifted her hand to heart. "Thank you for helping someone *begin again*." She reached out and the screen went black.

Sam resisted the urge to play the video again, to listen to her voice and let it carry him to unknown places. Instead, he grabbed

the leather notebook he kept in his back pocket and started
scratching words.

Moonflower,

linger...
this song inside me
sings itself; I am
a field plowed open, a
burning bridge. how
do I reach you from
here? I dream a song
of summer nights,
put your lips to my
sky and inhale the
music. the moon waits,
dipped in dew.

linger,
I have built
a temple of desire—
this season
of wanting grows
smooth and silken.
hunger is sweet
in silver light, but
breaks open with
sorrow. luminous sun
cloaks me in fire.

linger…
when will I touch you?

I will sing you to me.

His heart was pounding. A thought sparked. Before he could change his mind, he grabbed his phone and quick-dialed the familiar number.

"Hey. About time you called me back."

"Hello, sister. How do you feel about a GoFundMe concert in West Virginia?"

~

"Gil, how many times do I have to tell you to let me handle the booking? You don't do private parties, you know that. What in the world were you thinking? To add another show to this packed schedule? And in *three months*? And *that date*. It's right before the D.C. show. You need to be in top form for that one, it's one of our biggest. *Oddbird* is getting a lot of buzz. One of the reviewers on *Nashville Sound* even mentioned Grammy. We can't afford sloppy shows."

Scotty plopped down on the love seat in his cramped office and eyed Sam with frustration.

"What do you expect me to do with this?"

Sam smoothed a dark strand back into his ponytail. "Look, Scott, you don't have to *do* anything. All I need to do is show up. Me and a guitar. Mildred's handling the whole thing. Her people are event organizers. They've got this under control."

"You understand why I can't leave it at that, right? You are my hottest commodity right now. Did you hear me say the

G-word? I'm not kidding you. The critics love *Oddbird*. The rest of your shows for this year have sold out except the Ryman. And that one will be by the end of the week. I'm still getting calls about adding venues. We need to ride this wave."

Sam turned his back and pondered the view out the one small window. A large crow drifted onto the lamppost in the street below, wings held aloft like a parachute. An image flashed in his mind—a small boat, crowded and full of people who had nothing. A baby cried. It was his dream—this boat-cradle—the ocean holding him in her arms and gently rocking, rocking ...

"Gil. *Sam.*" His manager's voice was insistent. Sam turned back around to face him.

"Look, Scotty...this is important to me. You know I don't mess in 'issues,' but this time I have to."

Scotty held his eyes briefly before looking away. He drew in a deep breath and let his cheeks expand with a loud exhalation. "Fine. Get me the woman's contact information. What's her name, Millie? I don't want you involved in this. You are untouchable, okay? Instagram or no, it's not a good idea to interact with fans this way. Next thing you know you'll be booked at the circus."

Scotty sighed deeply again, put his elbows on his knees and grunted up from the cushion. Sam hesitated on the edge of the room as Scotty approached the mounds of paperwork burying his desk. He picked up an envelope, glanced at it, then tossed it in the trash can.

"Scott."

"Hmm?" Scotty didn't look up, just kept sorting.

"There's more."

Scotty lifted his eyes slowly. "What do you mean, Sam?"

"I need you to arrange a press conference. We're going to add more than one show."

~

"Hello, sister."

"Everything is going great. We have $10,000.00 in the GoFundMe already. Can you believe it? I told Mildred you're donating most of the expenses. We're having a Facetime meeting tomorrow to talk through details." Sher sounded distracted. Sam heard water running, the clank of pots and pans. "Mildred is great, do you know that? She's so easy to talk to. We talked for over an hour." He could hear the smile in her voice. "She's soooo ...humble? And wise. As soon as she starts speaking I feel a kind of peace come over me. Do you know what I mean?"

He did.

"Must be an Asian thing." She laughed at her own joke.

"Ha ha, very funny."

"Well, you're only *half* Asian. Or so we think, anyway. That explains the lack." She snorted. Dishes kept clanking in the background. He closed his eyes and pictured her—long red hair pulled back, phone cradled on her shoulder, hands busy in sudsy water. A pang inside bore the full weight of missing her.

"Mildred's only half Vietnamese, too. But, funny you should mention that. It's part of the reason I called, Sher."

"Oh, yeah? How so?"

"Do you still have the file? The one I gave you to keep for me?"

"You mean your adoption file." Her voice was flat.

"That's the one."

"I had Frank put it in a safe deposit box at the bank. Didn't trust keeping it around here. You never know what your nieces might use for an art project."

"Would you send it to me?"

The clanking of the pots stilled. He felt her caution.

"Why?"

"I'm not really sure yet. I just feel like I need to read through it again. Read the stuff about—you know, about the boat and the rescue and all that."

"Well, do you want me to send you just that? Or the entire file? It's pretty thick, you know."

"Send the whole thing. I want to look through it all again. See if there is something..."

"Something what, Sam? That we missed? We've pored over that thing."

He heard the edge in her voice. He couldn't understand why she was threatened by this. She and the girls were his only family now. And Frank too. She knew this. He closed his eyes and pushed back at the slip of annoyance beginning to take shape. He remembered her face the day he walked her into her kindergarten class the first time, their mother hovering behind. He was ten and she had clung to him like a quivering leaf on an autumn tree. "Don't leave me," she had pleaded. Even then, she had his heart. He could still see her five-year-old freckled face.

"Sam? What are you thinking?"

He blinked back to the present. "Nothing, little sister. Just wondering what I'd do without you. I would be one sad, lonely pup."

Sher sniffed on the other end of the line. "Don't you forget it, either," she said.

~

Sam could not remember ever *not knowing* he was adopted. He understood that he was "chosen." His parents picked him from the many other kids up for adoption. He was wanted and loved. Growing up, he had never questioned the circumstances that brought him into the Gillenwater family, even though he clearly looked very different than they did. The Gillenwaters, with their fair, freckled skin and copper-colored hair; their long, lanky limbs and easy smiles. Sam had never thought much about the contrast of his ebony hair and olive skin. And though he shared a blueness of eyes with his adopted family, the Gillenwaters' were an incandescent, laughing blue, while his were deep indigo—stormy and wild.

No, he had never cared to learn more about his birth family. That is, until their mother's death five years ago.

That was when he and Sher found the file. Both of his parents had been history professors and professional paper collectors. He and Sher went through document fatigue from the reams of papers that needed wading through while clearing out their parents' home. How many course curricula on the civilization of the ancient world could there possibly be? They found several lecture series from when Nan and Thom Gillenwater were both at UCLA. There were grade books and notes from students and buckets of index cards with citations on them. But when they opened the fireproof safe in the den, there was only one, bulging file within—a faded red elastic band barely holding it all together.

He stood behind a podium now, his right hand resting on that same dense file. Scotty had arranged for some of its contents, along with images and newsreel they'd found, to be projected onto the screen behind him. The small room was filling up, reporters buzzing with curiosity as their photographers edged closer to get the best shot. They were livestreaming on his Facebook page.

Sam swallowed. He did not have a prepared statement, despite Scotty's pleas. He was not expecting such a turnout—had underestimated the Grammy buzz. He waited for the bustle to slow, glanced at his watch, and cleared his throat. Everyone grew quiet and he was thankful for the screen behind him, drawing all eyes. Sher was in the front row, right beside Scotty, then his media team, and Brit, Dan, and Rob—the studio musicians he played with on *Oddbird*, who were now part of the tour.

Sam plowed forward. "For those of you who do not know me, my name is Sam Gillenwater. Most of you probably know me by 'Gil.' Maybe you've heard that my latest album, *Oddbird*, was mentioned on *Nashville Sound* last week as a possible Grammy nominee." Hoots and whistles rose up.

"Go, Gil!" someone offered.

Sam smiled. "Thanks. Thanks, guys. I'm grateful for my fans. The music business can be a lonely place, but you guys make it worthwhile." He looked up and grinned. "Sometimes."

Everyone chuckled.

"So. Yeah. My name is Sam Gillenwater. It's a name I've been proud to bear all my life. I've been making music a long time. The life of a musician is not as romantic as you might think. Sometimes you go from city to city to city for so long that there are days you wake up and can't remember where you are. Sometimes it feels like you don't have a home."

Sher gave him an encouraging look.

"So, yeah. I'm not good at speeches. Give me a guitar any day over a podium! But I've been doing a lot of thinking lately, and..." His breath caught. "Earlier this year I almost lost someone I care about, and it changed something in me. I can't explain it except to say that I'm realizing how fragile life can be, how little time we have, and I want my time to make a difference. Something beyond the music."

On the screen behind him an image of a newspaper article appeared. "The USS Edwin Phillips Rescues 438 Vietnamese Boat People," the headline read. Another article flashed. "Infant Born on Vietnamese Refugee Boat, Mother Dies."

Sam hesitated, unsure.

"Some of you may know I was adopted as an infant." A murmur traveled through the room. Apparently, most did not know.

"Thom and Nan Gillenwater were amazing parents. I had an ideal childhood. Five years ago, when my mother passed away, I found out that, were it not for the vision of commander Loren Wayne and the other crew members of the USS Edwin Phillips, things may have turned out differently for me."

The room was silent now, as its occupants tried to process what Gil was saying.

"I was born on a ramshackle 55-foot boat filled with 438 Vietnamese refugees. The boat was attacked by pirates, who stole the engine, took all the food and water, and raped some the women. When they were done, they pushed us out to sea to die. It was nearly a week before we were spotted by a crew member of the Phillips, somewhere off the coast of Malaysia. I was born during that week, adrift in the sea—one, tiny insignificant person. It was four years after the fall of Saigon, but many refugees were still fleeing Vietnam."

Sam looked intently into the faces of the crowd.

"At that time international law did not allow for the rescue of refugees, regardless of their condition. It took two days for the officers of the Phillips to get approval to take us aboard. During those two days, the crew helped us as much as they could, bringing food, water, medicine, whatever was needed. Finally, they were granted permission to take us aboard. Unfortunately, it was too late for my mother. I was orphaned the day I was born."

Sam patted the file on the podium.

"I read this story in here. I do not even know my mother's name. A woman who gave her life so her unborn child might know freedom." His voice cracked.

"Imagine if the crew had looked the other way. Because a lot of ships did just that. Left boatloads of refugees to whatever fate awaited them on the open sea. I do not know if all the adults would have perished aboard that tiny fishing boat, but I do know that a four-day old infant was unlikely to survive much longer. If not for the kind vision of strangers, I would not be here today."

He paused. Everyone was on the edge of their seat. Sher had tears streaming down her face.

"Five years ago, when I discovered the truth of my beginnings, I had no idea what to do with it. All I've ever wanted to do is make music. But with the current refugee crisis I feel like I've awakened. *I was a refugee.*"

Sam shifted on his feet.

"I've been looking for a way to say 'thank you.' For the opportunities I've been given. For the gift of doing what I love as a way of life. And now I think I've found one way to celebrate the beauty of the generosity shown to me, not only when I was a refugee, but throughout my life. My team and I have added a few shows to our tour in the next couple months. They're in smaller venues, more intimate settings than the regularly scheduled dates. One hundred percent of ticket sales from those shows will go to support organizations aiding refugees. We've been working with the IRC—the International Rescue Committee—and the UN Refugee Agency to work out details. Our final benefit show will be in September, in West Virginia. *This* is the show that inspired the additions. All funds from it are earmarked for a specific family being resettled in that area. We'll update you on Facebook as things develop. We've already set up a GoFundMe for people to donate. We'll give you the details about that in just a minute." The GoFundMe information flashed on the screen.

"I'm not going to take any questions right now because... because I hate stuff like this."

A chuckle passed through the room.

"But my manager and publicist, Scotty, and my little sister, Sher, who's in charge of fundraising, will be here for a while to field your questions." Scotty and Sher joined him at the podium. "Before I go I just want to say thank you. Thanks for listening, for supporting this effort, and for any ways you've ever shown kindness to someone who needs a new beginning. Where would this world be if we didn't help each other? Thank you."

A reporter in the second row stood up, "Sher! Sher! What do you think of all this? Will your brother try to find his birth family?"

Sher stepped up to the mic, catching Sam's eye. "I'll support Sam in whatever he wants to do. Right now, we just want to pay it forward."

Sam slipped into the background and walked quickly out the door. He did not look back. At the front of the building was a car waiting to take him home. He sank into the back seat, leaned his head back and closed his eyes.

Back at the house, he got a tall glass of water and went out to his watching chair. The doe and her fawns were back. All three had their legs folded neatly beneath them and were resting on the edge of forest grasses. The sun began to slip beneath the horizon, filling the sky with an amber hue. All the greens were lit golden. The heat from the day lingered, but something about the brink of twilight hinted at a dream of cooler nights. Fireflies winked in the trees.

~

His phone vibrated with a notification.

"**@giltheguitarman** Speechless. Your generosity is beautiful. I love your story. I'm grateful for everything that brought you where you are today."

His stomach did a tiny summersault. He took a sip of water, thought a second, typed a quick response.

"**@mildredsgarden** I had a moonflower muse. Thanks for the inspiration."

She sent him a private message.

"Still feeling overwhelmed by your story, Sam. Seriously. Can't wait to see you so I can hug your neck. Hope that's okay. You have the biggest heart. Thank you for all you're doing."

His skin tingled at the thought of wrapping his arms around Mildred. What was going on with him? He didn't even *know* this woman. He needed to get a handle on this. But he found himself typing a bold response.

"Never turned down a hug from a beautiful woman. You are beautiful from the inside out. Your generosity inspired mine. I should be thanking *you.* I am thanking you. Will it be okay if I hug you back?

He stared at the words. Punched "send" and leaned back.

A brief lapse of time. Then:

"Are you getting fresh with me? You just made this old maid's day. I'll take a hug from you anytime. Would indulge my longtime crush. You might go far with this new marketing strategy, considering the demographic makeup of your fan base ;).

Sam grinned. *Old maid?*

"Are you suggesting something other than the quality of my music as the reason behind my [insert sarcasm] vast following? Old maid, my left foot. It would be more like robbing the cradle. How young are you? I can't believe no one has won your hand yet. Why is that, do tell? We share a common cultural bond, even if I know little of the heritage. Perhaps that explains it."

He was enjoying this.

"You know I love your music. As for 'my hand,' that story is too complicated for Instagram. I have a feeling yours is too. We should talk. And, what do you mean, 'explains it?' Explains what?"

Sam drew in a sharp breath. What did he mean? *Explains why I can't stop thinking about you. Explains why the thought of you makes me lightheaded. Explains why I'm seized with fear and longing every time I see your name.*

"Explains…why I think we could be good friends."

Coward.

He stared at the empty response box. What else could he say? Who does this? Who tries to get to know a woman on Instagram?

The thing was, he felt like he already knew Mildred. Well, he knew he didn't *know* her. He didn't know her favorite food or flower. He didn't know if she'd ever been in love or wanted to have children. He didn't know if she liked chocolate or vanilla best. He didn't know her favorite movie or if she listened to classical music. Did she like horses? Jeans, or yoga pants? Did she have siblings? He could still smell her apple scent, lifted the fingers of his left hand as if it might still linger there after all these months. He inhaled a memory, closed his eyes and felt her hand in his.

Finally, the response came.

"Friends? Yes, that would make me happy. I think I know what you mean. I've always felt connected to you through your music, but these past couple weeks I've been beyond delighted at our shared passion to help refugees. It would make me dizzy with joy to call you friend. Good friend. And, Sam? I'm an American, through and through, but my mom tried to teach me a few things about her life in Vietnam. It was hard for her because it made her sad, but there were certain things that were so much a part of her she couldn't *not* share them with me. If ever you want to learn more about our Vietnamese heritage, I'd be glad to talk. For real. Face-to-face and in-person."

Beyond delighted. For a brief second the bottom dropped out of his world. He was falling, falling, spinning into another universe. He shook his head. Came back to earth.

"I would love that. I'll be seeing you in a few months for the concert. Maybe we could talk beforehand. Maybe I could visit when I have a couple days off in a row and scout the venue? The next few weeks are going to be a whirlwind."

"You just let me know. I would love a visit from you. Anytime. We can figure out details."

"Will do."

His cheeks were numb from grinning, heart pounding. The tips of his fingers tingled with expectation. Did he just invite himself to Mildred's home? And did she just say yes? He hovered above the tiny keyboard, waiting for her to rescind the offer. But she went silent after that. Just to be sure, Sam carried his phone around for the rest of the night. He obsessively checked his notifications as he stirred ravioli. He read the conversation over and over as he ate, wiped down the counters and table. Did he seem too eager? Was it tacky to ask why she wasn't married? He was seized with anxiety. Would she think him a weirdo?

By midnight he decided to give up this ghost-chase. It was crazy. It must be the Vietnam thing. But when he first met her, he had no idea about that. Yet, she sent his head spinning from the beginning. Was this kismet? He filled three pages in his poetry journal. Maybe he would at least get a song out of this.

> *I fall into the*
> *trespasser's dream;*
> *you lay yourself*
> *beneath me—together*
> *we will birth the sky;*
> *cover me in blue*

> *the light of morning*
> *stirs to life when you*
> *move; turn out the lamp,*
> *open the shades*

> *the gate swings wide,*
> *let me stay lost in this*
> *orchard with you, I*
> *will study the poetry*
> *written on your skin*

The *Oddbird* and Refugee* Tour

Fri, July 1	Chattanooga, TN	Tivoli Theatre
Sat, July 2	Knoxville, TN	Bijou Theatre
Wed, July 13	*Asheville, NC	Orange Peel

Refugee special guest: The Ibex

Fri, July 15	Birmingham, AL	The Lyric Theatre
Sat, July 16	Atlanta, GA	Variety Playhouse
Thurs, July 21	*Santa Cruz, CA	Rio Theatre

Refugee special guest: The Tenth Month

Fri, July 22	Santa Rosa, CA	Luther Burbank Center for the Arts
Sat, July 23	San Francisco, CA	The Fillmore
Wed, July 27	*Santa Barbara, CA	Lobero Theatre

Refugee special guest: Sajon Bellis and Hobbit Home

Fri, July 29	Los Angeles, CA	The Theatre at Ace Hotel
Sat, July 30	Seattle, WA	Moore Theatre
Fri, Aug 5	Hartford, CT	Infinity Hall
Sat, Aug 6	Providence, RI	Columbus Theatre
Thurs, Aug 11	*Portland, M	State Theatre

Refugee special guest: Tony Harrah and the Prohibition

Fri, Aug 12	Northampton, MA	Academy of Music Theatre
Sat, Aug 13	Boston, MA	Wilbur Theatre
Mon, Aug 15	*Burlington, VT	Higher Ground Ballroom

Refugee guest TBA

Fri, Aug 19	Albany, NY	Hart Theatre at the Egg
Sat, Aug 20	Ithaca, NY	State Theatre
Fri, Aug 26	New York, NY	Brooklyn Steele
Sat, Aug 27	New York, NY	le poisson rouge
Fri, Sept 2	Cincinnati, OH	Memorial Hall
Sat, Sept 3	Columbus, OH	Southern Theatre
Sun, Sept 4	Philadelphia, PA	Annenberg Center for the Performing Arts
Mon, Sept 5	Richmond, VA	The National
Wed, Sept 7	*Charlottesville, VA	Jefferson Theatre

Refugee special guests: The Lonely Bray, Tam Yearnke

Fri, Sept 9	*Charleston, WV	The Gardens

Refugee special guests: Ristach Swell & The Mountain Band

Fri, Sept 16	Washington DC	Lincoln Theatre
Sat, Sept 17	Charlotte, NC	Neighborhood Theatre
Sun, Sept 18	Saxapahaw, NC	Haw River Ballroom
Sat, Sept 24	Nashville, TN	Ryman Auditorium

~

Asheville

Sam stared at the hotel room ceiling in the first light of dawn. He couldn't stop smiling. The best. Show. Yet. It was standing room only, sold out. The Peel was a small venue, but still. They raised over $50,000 in their first Refugee Tour stop. The Ibex were the perfect partners. All their devotees made it one of the most exciting shows Sam had ever played. Only sheer exhaustion allowed him to get any sleep last night.

He knew he needed to get up and take a shower. They would be on the road to Birmingham in a couple of hours. But he wanted to savor this feeling. He watched a sliver of light sneak through the curtain and spill like water across the ceiling.

What do you call this feeling? He ran the movie of his life through his mind to find something to compare it to, something to name it. It was like the way he breathed after finishing a song. When all the lyrics and notes and chords came together perfectly. This feeling was a lot like creating. Almost like that, but something more.

He closed his eyes to the spilling light and felt his stomach fall. The bed cradled him close and started to spin. He sucked his breath in sharply and let a swirling world fill his consciousness. Two a.m. was never easy to recover from.

The swirling became images—memories flashing behind his eyes: that day at the bus stop after Tabitha Blake had called Sher a "fat-butted ostrich." How she cried in his arms. His favorite blue T-shirt soaked by tears. Then: at the hospital, the day Abby was born. Holding her in his arms. Those long-fingered baby hands. He thought his heart would break from her scent. And then: at the hospice house the day mom died. She'd asked him to play her soul into winter—to sing a never-ending lullaby. So he did.

He could count the times on two hands. This way of giving and giving and giving only to be surprised how much getting there is in the giving. This feeling? It resembled love.

He opened his eyes as the last images hovered. Mildred's face. His hand in hers.

On the Way to Birmingham

mildredsgarden "Sam!! 50k! Plus Sher says the GoFundMe is going crazy. I wish I could have been there last night."

giltheguitarman "It was all The Ibex. My fans don't go for standing room only, LOL. They like to sit in a cushy chair and sip frosty beverages like grown-ups. But I am so happy! Having you there is the only thing that would have made it better."

He felt the heat rising in his cheeks.

mildredsgarden "You are the sweetest. I'm so amazed at your generosity. And grateful. You make this world so beautiful."

giltheguitarman "Thanks, Moonflower. I can't wait to see you again."

Sam's phone buzzed right after he hit send. Someone from the agency.

"Yeah?"

"Gil? This is April."

"April?" Sam searched his mind for who in the world was April.

"Your social media manager?" Her tone was dry.

"Oh, yes! Of course! April. I'm sorry... just... late night last night."

"That's what I understand. Congratulations on the sell-out. Scotty is ecstatic. Even if none of the money comes to us."

"I just bet he is."

"Listen, I hope this isn't a bad time..."

"Not at all, we're still en route so I'm good. What can I do for you?"

"Well, I knew you'd be on the road a while, so I thought this might be a good time to, well, it's... just... um."

Sam waited. But the more April hem-hawed, the more nervous he got.

"What is it, April? You know me. I don't usually get too bent out of shape about things."

"It's not that, Gil. It's ... just ... um. Listen, do you ever read your Facebook messages?"

He never did. With all the political scrap going around he rather avoided Facebook. Too many words. Instagram was his thing. But somehow saying that to a social media manager didn't seem cool.

"Well, it's been awhile, with the tour and all, but sometimes?"

"Okay. Gotcha. Please don't get mad." Her voice had an edge of pleading.

"April, what's going on? You're starting to scare me."

"It's just that, I wanted to tell you right away, but you know Scott. He wanted to protect you and make sure this was all legit and not crazy fan stuff. So he hired a private detective and it turns out it all checks out ..."

"What checks out? Private detective? What are you talking about?" Sam closed his eyes and pictured Della's latest ballet ensemble. He didn't know if she could dance but that child sure looked cute in a tutu.

"I don't think I should tell you. I think you need to read it for yourself. So I'm telling you, go to your Facebook page and look at Messenger. We've cleaned up all the other crazy, off-the-wall messages. When you are done reading, call Scotty. He has the master plan."

"But—"

April hung up.

Sam took a deep breath and exhaled noisily. "Okay."

He really didn't need any more distractions. He glanced at his notifications.

mildredsgarden "I'm excited to see you too."

He let himself feel a wave of pleasure then glanced at his watch. Was it really only 11:00 a.m.? Thinking about Mildred made him hungry. He would check the Facebook messages but first things first. He needed fortification.

Sam preferred to ride alone. Just he and his driver, Renault. He used to insist on driving himself—that was back in the days of the Toyota minivan. He put a lot of miles on that thing. Even rebuilt the engine once. But a couple of years ago when things started getting better financially, Scotty talked him into using the travel time for writing and what he called "performance strategy." All the techs, other musicians and equipment were on the bigger bus and in its trailer but Renault and Sam stayed under the radar in a smaller conversion van. It was a comfortable ride with a reclining sofa and swivel bucket seats (what Scotty called "the conversation area"—mainly used for conversation only when he rode along), satellite TV, and built-in ice box. But sometimes Sam still missed that old Toyota minivan. He did appreciate the sofa, though, upon which he currently reclined—guitar across his lap. Seatbelt on, of course.

Renault seemed to be part of the package when they bought the thing. Sam had no idea where Scotty found him, but he was glad of it. He and Renault had reached a comfort level with just the right combination of silence and conversation. Renault was trustworthy and kind and Gil knew most of the stories from his life. They'd been stranded along the road together more than once—snowbound, flooded out, and just about any other travel crisis imaginable. Once, when a tornado blew out their show in

Missouri, Renault helped him assemble an impromptu acoustic set at a roadside park. The residents of the little town needed a distraction and they had no place to be.

Sam leaned forward.

"Hey, Renault. You hungry?"

The younger man glanced at Sam in the rear-view mirror. Tired brown eyes.

"I could eat."

"Let's get off at the next exit. Where the hell are we, anyway?"

"Almost to Athens."

"Mmm. You know anyplace good to eat in Athens?"

"What you in the mood for?"

"I've got the hungries. A juicy burger sounds good."

"Mama's Boy is the best. They've got a good pimento cheese burger. But the biscuits are famous. Ever been there?"

"No but that sounds like it'd hit the spot. Maybe even with fries."

He glanced down at his phone and saw another notification from Mildred.

mildredsgarden "Sam, do you mind if I call you? Sher passed along your number. I hope that's okay. I promise not to be a weird fangirl ;). I have a couple questions about the amphitheater I think you might be able to help with."

Sam swallowed nervously. Could he have a conversation with Mildred? A real conversation? In some ways it had been easy to hide behind social media. He didn't have to think on his feet, could ponder his words before responding. For someone who tended to be a slow processer, this was a big deal. But how could he refuse? This was Mildred. His heart had been longing for a deeper connection with her for months now. Besides, it was only business, right?

He took a deep breath and typed.

giltheguitarman "No worries. I'd love to help. We're almost to Athens where we're stopping for lunch but can talk now if you'd like."

mildredsgarden "Great! Calling."

~

Her voice was a song, and after they hung up he couldn't stop humming. Despite the out-of-body feeling Mildred evoked in him, he was able to hold it together to answer her questions. She wanted advice about using the amphitheater to host regular musical artists and other theatrical events. After some discussion, they agreed she would Facetime him later—after lunch—and show him the area they were developing. She wanted his thoughts on layout and design, based on some of the venues he'd played.

And then Sam had an idea. He tried to make his voice sound casual. "So, we have a little break after Atlanta. Five days before the show in Santa Cruz. I was thinking about your offer—you know, to talk about our Vietnamese heritage. I would really love to know more... about your mom, and what she taught you and so, I was thinking—if it's not too much trouble—maybe I could fly out there. Take a look at the amphitheater site in person and visit with you some." He took a deep breath.

Mildred was silent, just long enough to make him regret the suggestion.

"But if it's too much—I mean, I know you're still just getting started with the business and you probably don't have a lot of time to—"

"No, no," Mildred interjected. "I was just surprised, that's all. Cindy and I would love to have you. I meant what I said about sharing my story. And we always have rooms at the ready. We would be…delighted if you came for a visit."

Sam couldn't resist. "Will you fluff my pillow?"

Mildred laughed stiffly. "Personally," she said. There was a pause. "Look, Sam, I need to help Cindy set up for an event we're hosting tomorrow. When you make your arrangements, just let me know the details. We'll pick you up at the airport and bring you straight to The Gardens."

He felt the shift in her. Her warmth walled off.

"Are you sure? I don't want to inconvenience you—"

Again, a pause. Then, "Not at all, Sam. I think," she hesitated. "I think I would very much like to see you again."

His heart did a flipflop. "And I, Mildred, would very much like to see you."

"Okay then. Just let me know the details and I'll see you soon."

"See you soon, Mildred."

He hung up. The world seemed so lovely. Sunshine was flooding in the windows and the scenery they bypassed was all happy blues and greens.

Sam began to hum. He was going to see Mildred in three days.

~

Sam was still humming when he opened the Facebook Messenger app. Might as well see what April was all worked up about…

Dear Sir,

My name is Wren Pham and I live in Bonita, California. A friend who knows my family well sent me the YouTube link to the news conference you gave last month and I had to write.

My mother, Kay Nguyen, was fourteen years old in May of 1979, when she and her older sister Thia were put on a boat filled with other fleeing Vietnamese. Their story is one that my mother speaks of often and with great love. See, Thia was very pregnant when they left. She gave birth to a baby boy on the open sea. The group of refugees was rescued by the USS Edwin Phillips Aunt Thia died shortly after she had the baby.

Do you see why I knew I must contact you? I do not know if you will receive this message, cousin, but I am in earnest to reach you. My mother has been ill with cancer and though she is doing well at this moment, she has stopped all treatments and her doctors tell us it is only a matter of time. They have given her six months to a year to live. I have not told her about your story, for I fear to get her hopes up—and to not have them realized would be too much. She loved Thia very much, and to see her sister's son before she dies would be a blessing. Is there a way to make this happen? My mother still has many good days, and though travel may be difficult, it is doable. But I do not know for how long. Please let me know what you think, for I know my words may be a heavy stone cast onto the sea of your life.

You may message me here or please call my cell phone at (619) 543-1232.

Your cousin,
Wren Pham

~

Renault had heard enough of Sam's side of the conversation with Scotty, regarding the Facebook message, to know to be quiet all the way to Birmingham.

Sam sat alone on the reclining couch, fingering his cell phone. What to do first? Sher? Should he talk to Wren before upsetting his sister?

He thought Sher would be okay with everything, even excited for him, as long as he kept her in the conversation. But at this point, did he even know what to tell her about all this? He felt like he needed to talk to his new-found cousin—if for no other reason than to confirm she was real. It felt ... impossible. Impossible after thirty-seven years of living that he could find his family. That there were people in the world who shared his blood.

He had a family.

He blinked and shook his head. Of course, he had a family. Sher and Abby and Della and Frank were his family. But people who shared his blood were alive. That was something he'd never even allowed himself to think about. Sam sighed, stretched his legs and stuck his phone in his back pocket. He would do what he always did when having trouble deciding: take a nap.

He didn't know how long he'd been asleep when he heard a soft chiming. Sam blinked awake. The road was still scrolling along beneath them. Dappled sunlight played across the seat. Maybe he was dreaming. He closed his eyes.

But the chiming persisted. With a start, he realized someone was trying to Facetime him. He fished his phone out of his back pocket, stared at the screen, and hit the "accept" button.

"Mildred?"

She beamed. "I'm sorry to bother you again, Sam. I hope I haven't caught you at a bad time. I just got off the phone with Sher and we thought you might like some good news. We've gotten another corporate sponsor! For $5,000.00!"

He smoothed his unruly hair away from his face. "That's great, Mildred. $5,000.00. Wow."

Her brow knit together and a tiny crescent-shaped indentation formed between her eyes. Sam felt his heartbeat accelerate slightly.

"Are you okay?"

"Oh, yeah. Fine. I was just taking a nap."

"Oh! Did I wake you? I'm sorry."

"It's fine, Mildred. I'm glad to see your face." He struggled to sound casual.

She smiled and looked away from the camera. When she returned her gaze, that little moon waxed between her eyes again. "I-I'm glad to see yours too." There was an awkward pause and Sam cleared his throat—searching for words. Any words.

Mildred gave her head a little shake and the worry left her eyes. "Hey, do you want to walk up to The Glasshouse with me right now? Is this a good time?"

"Sure, if it's good for you."

Mildred started walking.

"Let's go! Cindy and I are really excited about the possibility of being a regular music venue. Since it was inspired by you, we might even name it the Sam Gillenwater Soundstage." She teased, smiling a crooked smile, revealing that dimple again.

Sam felt a little light-headed and a warm blush began to creep up his neck and into his cheeks. There was a meaningful pause. Mildred stopped moving and frowned, diamond between her eyes. "Sam? Are you okay? You seem...distracted."

Sam felt tingly all over and, to his wonder, he felt tears begin to form. His throat felt tight and he coughed uncomfortably.

"Sam?"

He cleared his throat. "Well, actually, Mildred, I just found out something that's rocking my world a little. And because of this thing, I'm not sure I'll get to come to West Virginia next week after all. I'm not sure of anything. In fact, I could use a friend's ear right now."

Disappointment, then—was it relief he saw on her face?

"Hold on," she said. "I'm going to take you to the gazebo."

She walked him through a busy kitchen, clanging dishes and fast-scurrying servers dodging their pass-through. He heard the screen door screech as she pushed it open, then bang shut behind her. They walked up a narrow path, past tall, loping flowers. "This is the white flower garden," she said, showing him various pale blooms as they passed by. When he saw the sunlight glimmer on the petals, Sam felt that wild stirring he always felt when viewing her Instagram, but more intense and dreamlike. "We're walking up what I used to call Flat Rock Path when I was a little girl. I named it after these natural stone pavers my dad excavated from the Blackwater River. Original, huh?" She flipped the phone over so Sam could see the smooth, white stones. He caught a glimpse of her feet, naked and slender. Robin's egg blue toenails. A warm glow began inside him. The line created by the length of her toes was a perfect descending angle, the ball of her foot culminating in a sweetly curved inset, gently rounded heel and shapely ankle. He was speechless but he needn't have worried. Before a response seemed necessary, Mildred piped up, "Let's take a quick detour. I want to show you something." She picked up the pace, jogged off Flat Rock and through some yellow grasses.

Sam was curious. "What is it?"

"Here!" She peeked into the camera before pointing it upward. "My tree!"

"Your tree?"

"Yes! Isn't it beautiful? It's an almond tree, hardy. My dad planted it and its mate for me when I was ten years old. He said it was because I was so nutty." She turned the camera back on her face. "You should see it in the spring. Full of amazing pink blossoms." She showed him the tree again. "Now it's just...green." But Sam saw it. The tree filled with lacy pink blooms, spilling over every arc of every branch, creating an undulating, flowering sea.

"It's beautiful."

She smiled. "It's very special to me. But enough about me. Let's get back on the path." Once again, the golden greens, then the stone walkway.

"Mildred."

"Umm-hmm?"

"When I finally do get to visit, will you give me a tour of the property? All of it?"

She turned the camera back on the full moon of her face. "Of course! It's one of my favorite things, to share all this. If you really want to see the entire acreage, though, it will take more than a couple days."

Sam pondered this.

"I'll just have to make sure we have plenty of time together then."

It was her turn to blush. She lowered her eyes then smiled

into his before she turned him outward again. "Here we are." She scanned the little lake and the iron gazebo in front of it, then nestled into the cushions on a chaise lounge and focused on Sam. "This is where we want to build the stage—but we can talk about that in a bit. What's on your mind?"

They talked for forty-five minutes. Under the warmth of Mildred's kindness, Sam felt his excitement kindle. The wonder of meeting his mother's sister and the possibility of hearing the story of his family began to fill him.

"Thia," he told her. "My mother's name was Thia."

Mildred was a good listener. And she asked questions that helped point a way through. By the time they said goodbye Sam had a plan. And he had promised to Facetime Mildred again after the show.

"It will be late," he told her.

"I'll wait up."

She did. After they talked that night, he promised to Facetime her again the next night. And the next. And the next after that.

Begin with me, barefoot,
under the almond tree;
child of yesterday
pink dream of blossoms;
grasses soft under the temple of
your slender feet. Unstring
the day and let me remember
five toes angled perfectly, each
topped with a blue moon.

MILDRED

[june-july]

She couldn't sleep.

What a night. What a night, what a night, what a night! Her brain would not slow down. She still couldn't believe she had met Sam Gillenwater! He had only been her favorite Indy artist since before there was even such a thing as an Indy artist. And she had met him. Held his hand, even.

She cupped her hands and lifted them to her nose, as if she could scoop the scent of him out of the air. It was gone now, but she remembered. It was like the ocean, like the sky—clean and wild and...sweet. Yes, that was it. Sweet. A warm-sugar breeze. She rubbed her thumb over her fingers, remembering the callouses on the tips of his—all those years of strumming strings. His hand was soft in hers—his touch gentle. She wrapped her arms around herself and let herself wonder what those hands would feel like all over her skin. She hadn't allowed herself to think such thoughts for so long now. *But this isn't real,* she told herself. *No danger here. Just a harmless fantasy to distract me from my lonely little life.*

"Did you see the way he looked at you?" Cindy had asked. "He could not take his eyes off you!"

Mildred had laughed and joked about her rock star appeal. But. Sam Gillenwater! She had loved his music for so long. Who knew he was so cute in person? And those eyes. She felt her stomach dip a little at the memory of how he held her in all that blue. Was she crazy? But she had felt something. Like an invisible string twined around them and between them, inexplicably pulling them toward one another.

Mildred shifted Pete from his warm nest under the covers (honestly, that dog!) and leaned to grab her phone from the bedside table. She sank back into her oversized pillow, let the screen light up the darkness. So much for sleep hygiene. She couldn't help herself. She pulled up her camera roll to have one last look. Maybe this would help. A photograph lullaby. Fodder for sweet dreams. Just one more look.

Their hands were entwined and he was looking down—his face soft, tender. On an impulse, she pulled up her Instagram feed and added the photo.

"What a thrill to meet **@giltheguitarman** at #mountainstage tonight! Brought out the fangirl in me." She typed it quick, before she could change her mind. When the photo popped up, she scrolled through her home feed and liked a few images from friends, then ended up back at the shot she'd just posted.

With a start she realized Gil had already liked the picture. Underneath her comment was his:

@mildredsgarden "The pleasure was all mine."

The words made her dizzy with joy. A notification popped up: "**giltheguitarman** started following you." Without thinking, she tapped "follow back." "Requested" popped up.

Oh, shoot! His was a private account. She felt a tiny cringe. He probably didn't want his fans creeping on him here. Briefly, she wondered if there was a way to withdraw her request. But she let herself sit with the discomfort. What was that Father Mike had said? *You do not let yourself be vulnerable.* Well, who did? This made her feel like a silly school girl. That deep terror of the secret crush revealed. The "what-if-he-doesn't-like-me?" kind of fear. Ugh. Another reason to stick with her plan to swear off men forever.

With a heavy groan she shifted Pete with her legs. "Sorry, boy. Mom needs a breather."

Mildred slid out from under the covers, dropping her phone into one of the pockets of her satiny PJ top. Petey wiggled his stout body up from the middle of the bed, leaving the warm spot behind. He nudged his pink nose into the open and watched her cross the room to the window.

Mildred released the latch on the old casing and pushed its wooden frame up. Her reno team had painted the trim throughout the entire house just last month and the fresh white made the frames a little sticky. Absently, she rubbed her hand over the glossy smoothness of the sill. The screens she ordered would be ready to install next week. She thought of the window boxes waiting in the barn—newly painted and ready for placement. Every window on the front of the old farmhouse would soon have its own flower garden. She imagined impatiens in the summer, tulips and hyacinths come spring, pansies in the fall.

There was still much to do to make the property ready for the grand opening. She didn't mind. It was the kind of work that made her come alive: dipping her hands into soil, planning for seasons of beauty. Helping her forget...other things. She smiled as she remembered how frustrated her mother used to get when she would run out to the garden with her dad instead of helping with the kitchen work. Planting and growing. These were the things she understood. The world of love might be a mystery, but she could grow a tulip. There were rules about these things—when to place the bulb in the soil, how deep to plant, how to fertilize for optimal bloom. Planting and growing made sense. The more time and love you invested, the more the reward. But *men?* That world of love had no rules. Mildred shook her head and came back to the present. With Cindy in charge of the kitchen and the property being her bailiwick—she knew they couldn't fail. It was a dream come true for both of them.

Mildred sighed and leaned through the window. This wasn't where she thought she'd be at this point in her life. So many things shifted from her young-girl dreams. She tilted her head back and looked up at the night sky. The moon's full round eye shimmered on the tip of Ruffner Mountain, blinding the stars.

She smiled in the darkness of her room and felt a small buzz in her pocket. She almost didn't check the notification, didn't want to lose the sky and the moon and the moment. But when she pulled her phone out she saw "**giltheguitarman** accepted your follow request." She leaned toward the sky. She remembered Gil's hand in hers. His ocean eyes. She didn't go back to bed for the longest time.

~

Mildred opened her eyes with a start. A quick glance out the window told her the sun was already climbing the sky. She swung her legs over the side of the bed and ran to the shower. She heard Petey jump off the bed behind her. So much to do today! The landscape architect was coming for the final walkthrough at ten. Honestly, that man! She'd never had a more difficult time getting someone to listen to what she wanted. She needed him to make a few major last-minute changes. The opening was next week, for Pete's sake. And he hadn't even mapped out the perennial bed. There were some perennials planted, for sure, but she'd explained over and over how they needed these flowers to be rotational, replacing themselves so she would have a plentiful supply for cut-flowers. What self-respecting bed and breakfast did not have fresh flowers? He kept warning her about "summer heat" and "dry season" and everything she already knew. The timing wasn't great but most dream-chasing never was.

She decided not to wash her hair and did her best to keep it out of the water. It took so long to dry. Maybe it was time to cut it off. Maybe she was getting too old for all this hair. She sighed as she turned off the water and grabbed a towel. She didn't have much time. Pete watched her from the patchwork chair in the corner. "Hello, Baby!" She reached down to scratch the beagle's tummy. The dog rolled over to give her better access. "It's hard getting up this morning, isn't it, boy?" She bent over and gave his happy nose a kiss. Pete lifted his face, wagged his tail gently. Mildred grabbed the jeans draped over the back of the chair and pulled them over long legs and slim torso. Two days worn, already soft for the wearing. In the closet, she rummaged through her simple tops and chose a soft button up. She pulled her hair back in a ponytail—damp tendrils curling uncooperatively around her face—grabbed her camera bag, and headed to the kitchen, Pete trailing.

The scent of something cinnamony met her in the downstairs hallway. Cindy was already at work, testing recipes and training the kitchen staff. Mildred pushed open the heavy farmhouse door to find them all sitting around the big wooden table, helping themselves to a platter of scones.

"Well, good morning, sleepyhead!" Cindy didn't even look up from the plate she was dressing. She placed a scone on the bone white china and drizzled a sugary glaze over its top. Then she artfully painted glaze circles around the biscuit. When she was finished, she plucked a couple mint leaves from a sprig soaking in a vase in the middle of the table and tucked them in under the scone. She held the plate out to Mildred.

"Tell me what you think."

Mildred looked at Cindy's handiwork. A shame to eat such loveliness. She set the camera bag on the table and unzipped the top.

"Hold that thought," she said, as she took the plate from Cindy's hands. She set it on the edge of the knotted pine table, moved the vase of mint to twelve o'clock, then looked around. "I'll take that," she said, removing an ivory mug of breakfast tea from a young woman's (*I think her name is Alice,* she thought) grasp. She set the ceramic at two o'clock. Then she pulled a chair up and looked down at her still life. "Perfect." She snapped a couple shots, rearranging to get just the right fit.

When she looked up, all eyes were on her. "May I have my tea back now?" the young-woman-who-might-be-Alice asked. Everyone broke into laughter. Mildred smiled and gingerly nudged the mug across the table with the toe of her shoe. She hopped off the chair to face a Cindy with her hands on her hips.

"What? We're going to need that shot next week for Instagram!"

Cindy raised her eyebrow.

"You'll thank me later."

"Look, are you gonna eat this scone or not? 'Cause I've got plenty of other takers if you're not interested."

Mildred carefully picked up the biscuit, avoiding the glaze

with her fingers. The cinnamon sugar melted on her tongue, flooding her with goodness.

"Oh, my!" she said, mouth full. "Amazing! How did you get such...such...cinna-goodness?"

"Cinna-goodness? Seriously? Is that the best you can do?"

Mildred dipped the corner of the scone into the drizzled glaze. "Cindy. This is perfection."

Cindy glowed. "Family recipe. With a couple of tweaks from yours truly." She winked. "Are you sure you like it? I'm thinking the scones will be our signature breakfast item. We'll have the omelets, of course, and fresh fruit, and daily specials, but this would be the one thing we always have on the menu."

Mildred lifted the fork and scraped the rest of the glaze off the plate. After freeing the fork of its sweet cargo, she pointed it at Cindy.

"Excellent idea."

Cindy smiled. Pete nudged Mildred's leg and wagged his butt until she moved to a canister on the baker's rack nearby. One scoop filled the dog's waiting dish with breakfast. She took the water dish and filled it with fresh water. "There you go, boy!"

Pete looked at the dry dog food, then at Mildred. When she didn't move he shifted his gaze to Cindy and pawed at her leg. Cindy stooped down and took his face in her hands. "I'm sorry, boy," she said, to his sad brown eyes. "No scones for you."

Standing back up, Cindy glanced at Mildred.

"You look a little rough. Trouble sleeping? Too much excitement? So much for our She-Woman-Man-Haters Club."

Mildred couldn't help smiling. "That full moon was shining straight into my dreams. How could a woman sleep with such a bright light?"

"I wonder."

Mildred set the plate down on the table and gingerly licked the stickiness from her thumb. "I'll be out on the grounds most of the day if you need me. Speaking of man-haters—and I'm still a card-carrying member, so don't go abandoning our pledge— Jim the landscape guy should be here in half an hour. We're going to look everything over one more time so I can give him a list of things we still need done."

"Oh? Jim is coming?" Cindy reached up and smoothed her hair. Mildred tried not to smirk. "Okay. We're making avocado BLTs for lunch. There will be extras if Jim wants to join us. I'll ring the bell when it's ready."

"Yum! You won't need to call me twice. And I'll make sure to invite Jim." Mildred winked at Cindy's reddened cheeks then left through the back kitchen door, Pete jogging behind, nose to the ground.

~

Cindy sat on the loveseat in the nook by the south window, a three-ring binder in her lap. Index cards were spread out on the coffee table in front of her and pieces of yellowed paper covered with her grandmother's long scrawl were strewn around. She had a glazed look in her eye.

"Whatcha doin'?" Mildred asked, plopping down and bouncing Cindy a little with the landing.

"Menu plans."

"Hmm. Sounds fun."

"It started out being. Now I'm just exhausted. If I have to do one more triple or quadruple conversion, my head might explode. These recipes are all for a family of six. Not thirty-five paying guests."

Mildred patted Cindy's leg. "You're doing great work, you know. That cinnamon scone was a-mazing this morning. And lunch was scrumptious. Jim couldn't say enough about how good his sandwich was. Have I said how glad I am we're in this together?"

Cindy squeezed Mildred's hand without taking her eyes off the recipes in front of her. "Thanks, Mil. You know I feel the same. It's just going to be a bundle of crazy until we get things up and running smoothly. I know I can't anticipate every bump in the road but I sure am going to try." She paused for a second, then, "Did Jim really like his sandwich? I put extra avocado on his. He loves avocado, you know. How'd it go this afternoon?"

Mildred threw her head back against the plush pillowed top of the loveseat. "Yes, he loved the sandwich. And I don't know why you two don't just go out. You're both very obviously interested in each other. It's not like you haven't known him for years."

Cindy tried to protest but Mildred held up her hands. "And maybe you could talk some sense into that man. Talk about bumps in the road. He's a hard worker, that's for sure, but he has absolutely no imagination! I can't seem to get him to understand my vision for this place. I wish I had only hired him to do the labor and not the design. We're stuck with his crew for now, but I'm going to be on the lookout for someone who'll catch my vision and fly with it. I feel very frustrated right now."

"That bad?"

"He talks to me like I'm a first-grader. Not someone who has grown up and worked around flowers all her life. I've shown him all the plans for every bed I've mapped out. He has a reason for every single one as to why he can't do it the way I want it."

"Well, he does have a cute butt."

Mildred rolled her eyes. "I've never noticed. Can't get past his condescension. I mean, really, he's a nice guy, C. And he's fine with design if you want the typical symmetrical beds and standard plants. But he just doesn't know what to do with me. You, on the other hand, I'm sure he has ideas. But there is one thing you should know about him."

"And what's that?"

"He doesn't like dogs."

They both looked over at Petey, snoring in his favorite sunspot.

"For Pete's sake."

"For Pete's sake."

~

"Have you read it yet?"

"No. I'm too nervous about it. Usually they take my words out of context and just paint me as a bleeding-heart without a brain. I thought I'd have my coffee first."

Mildred carried the pot to the wooden table. Cindy pushed the cream pitcher toward her, the Sunday paper underneath.

"Bill did a good job. He only mentioned your 'activist' history in the beginning."

Mildred glanced down.

"What? Are you serious? 'Local activist?' Come on. Participating in a couple demonstrations makes me an 'activist'?"

Cindy chuckled. "Well, I'd say it's been more than a couple over the years. Between mountaintop removal and how vocal you were after the Fridays for Future marches…"

"All right, all right. But I am never the leading voice. I just lend my support."

"And the news people always love to interview you because you are so passionate and articulate and have all your teeth. Not to mention the Ruffner name. But it was really that mountain top removal protest clip that made it to *The Today Show* what earned you the 'activist' name."

"I don't want to talk about it. My hair looked awful in that clip."

"You should have flown up there and let them interview you in person like they wanted."

"It was the principle of the matter. No capitalizing on our ruined earth. We ended up getting more publicity because I didn't go. Daryl Hannah would never come back if I was the star."

Cindy raised her eyebrows. "Are you serious?"

Mildred laughed. "Nah. She doesn't care about that stuff, for Pete's sake."

"For Pete's sake." Cindy ruffled the paper again. "Just read. It's great publicity. I've already taken ten reservations for dinner on opening night."

"Ten? Wow!" Mildred picked up the paper with one hand and sipped coffee with the other. She read aloud.

Local Activist Settles Down, Opens Bed and Breakfast
By Bill Lynch

Mildred Ruffner is passionate about the hills of West Virginia. The Charleston native made national news in 2009 when she was arrested alongside actor Daryl Hannah at a mountaintop removal protest in Raleigh County. While still a strong supporter of environmental causes, the main focus of Ruffner's land reclamation lately has been her family's 200-year-old farm. She and lifelong friend—now business partner—Cindy Newton, have been renovating and restoring the 100-acre property for two years, in preparation for the opening of The Gardens, a bed and breakfast and event venue. Newton, a trained pastry and culinary chef, is in charge of the kitchen and Ruffner has taken on the grounds of her family homestead.

"Do not ask Mildred to have anything to do with food except eat it," Newton joked, during the course of our several hours together on a Sunday afternoon. "But she's brilliant with the growing things. We've had this dream for a long time—a way to marry my gifts and hers—and it feels surreal that it's finally coming true."

The two women gave me a tour of the newly restored house, featuring a huge wrap-around porch decked with inviting rocking chairs ("I love sitting out here when I have a cake in the oven," said Newton), twelve private suites ("One for each of the ten children my great-great-great grandfather—Thomas Ruffner—had, plus he and my grandmother's bedroom and a guest suite," Ruffner said), a recent addition that hosts an upscale restaurant ("This addition brings the farmhouse into the twenty-first century," Newton gushed), a cozy sunroom ("Petey's favorite room," Newton and Ruffner said, simultaneously, referring to the resident hound dog), a sprawling second story library with a glass window-wall overlooking the gardens ("Dad loved to read," said Ruffner), and numerous details that breathe comfort and care into every nook and cranny. Ruffner and Newton hired Teays Valley design firm Yeager Interiors to give their inn authentic farmhouse charm, combined with modern comforts.

After touring the house and a quick lunch of gazpacho with a rustic crostini drizzled in olive oil (excellent!), Ruffner walked me through several of her gardens. She explained the footprint for grounds was an expansion of her mother's original gardening plans.

"When my mother left her birth country of Vietnam as a young bride and made the United States her new home, the only thing she brought with her was a love for all growing things," says Ruffner. "Well, that, and her cousin, who I called uncle, *Van Minh*. Together they created these gardens of the four *qui,* or the four seasons, so they would always have a little piece of their homeland with them."

We ate dessert (Newton's Aunt Effie's famous Banana Cake with Caramel Icing—to die for) in The Glasshouse, home to Anya Ruffner's extensive orchid collection, as well as many other rare specimens.

"Mother befriended Dr. Beck, the director of The C. Fred Edwards Plant Conservatory that is part of the Huntington Museum. Together they shared a passion for orchids that benefitted both of their stock," Ruffner explained. "Dr. Beck has been very generous in helping me preserve and add to mother's smaller collection."

Mildred trailed off and read the rest of the article silently. Cindy studied her friend's face, watched her natural buoyancy sink into deep waters. The rise of the little half-moon on her brow always betrayed her thoughts of her mother.

Mildred folded the paper and gave a distracted smile. "Bill did a good job, you're right. I'm glad they included our web address."

Cindy reached over and rubbed Mildred's shoulder. "I know you miss her. I do too. She would be so proud of what you've done here, Mildred."

Mildred's face crumpled and she drew in a shaky breath.

"I miss them both, so much, C. I can't stop thinking about them lately. The way dad would tuck me in at night—the roughness of his hands and the way his beard tickled my nose. How he smelled of grass and earth and everything living. How he answered my crazy questions about life and the world after the lights went out. His endless, boundless patience. And mom. So soft and good. She would hug me with her entire body, you know? Just cover me up with her whole self. It felt so right to be wrapped up in her arms. She smelled of rose-water. I miss how there wasn't a green thing she didn't stop to touch. How she loved beauty and the way she brushed my hair."

She turned to her friend. "I so wish they could be here. I so wish they could see all this."

Cindy wrapped her arms around Mildred. "I know, Mil. I know."

~

She almost missed his comment. The rains had slowed to a drizzle and Mildred was in the old horse barn mucking out some sludge from the small leak the roof gave way to last summer. No horses now, just four dairy cows, the grain for the cows and chickens, all the organic plant foods, and several pieces of old farm equipment. It was really a glorified storage shed. Only now it was dangerously close to being underwater.

"I really need a roofer friend," she muttered as she squeegeed the floor clean. Meredith, her favorite milk-cow, gazed dolefully over the stall. "And just what are you staring at?" Mildred asked the big brown eyes. "Oh, alright. I know what you want." She leaned the squeegee against the wall and headed over. "Here you go," she said as she firmly scratched the wide expanse between the cow's eyes. Meredith leaned into her massage. "Why are you such a big sweetie? Hmm? Tell mama. Why are you so sweet?" She kissed the white nose.

Mildred sighed and sat down on a bale of hay beside the stall. There was so much to do. Still. And she was hungry. It was a little early for lunch but she was hankering for some of Cindy's chicken salad. With extra grapes and walnuts. She pulled her phone out of her pocket to text C about her craving. Before she could compose the message, a notification popped up.

giltheguitarman commented on your post.

Her tummy did a little loop. *What in the world is wrong with me?* She tapped the notification.

@mildredsgarden "Congrats on your new venture, Moon-flower. Next #mountainstage, save me a room."

The thought of Sam Gillenwater under her roof was too wonderful to ponder. She tapped a quick response.

@giltheguitarman "You have an open invitation. Any. Time."

She took a deep breath and added:

"I'll fluff the pillows even."

It made her blush. Would he think she was suggesting something more? Was she?

She waited for a response. But after ten minutes she looked

over at Meredith. "I guess it's back to mucking, girl."

~

"Mildred! Hurry up, we're going to be late!"

Cindy banged on her bedroom door. Mildred ran the brush through her long hair one more time, grabbed her brown silk scarf and tied it around her neck as she sprang for the door.

"I know, I know. I'm sorry. I got carried away with the window boxes. I didn't have time for a shower." She sniffed under her armpits. "Do I smell?"

Cindy rolled her eyes. "You're the one who wanted to do this. We have a million other things we need to take care of, but we can't miss one of Father Mike's guest speakers."

"Cindy, it's Zahura Rasho. Don't you want to hear her story first-hand? You know I couldn't put her book down when I read it last year. But lately, I've been so wrapped up in getting ready for The Gardens' opening, I haven't even thought about the refugees. I need to hear this. I need reminded that the world is bigger than my little corner in it."

They were walking and talking—quickly—to the old Ford pickup truck parked by the barn. Mildred swung the driver's side door open and slid behind the wheel. Cindy climbed in beside her.

"I know, Mildred, but do we really have time for a human-interest project? Our little corner of the world is commanding a heckuva lot of attention right now. I'm just saying. Let's get settled into this. When things take off, we can help Father Mike all you want."

"Who said anything about a project? I'd just like to meet her.

I want to hear what she has to say."

Cindy stared at the winding dirt road rolled out like a ribbon before them. The sun spilled a rosy hue over the horizon and the trees swayed with an unseen breeze. "Umm-hmm," she said. "Right."

Mildred glanced at her out of the corner of her eye. "Have you been keeping up with the Instagram account?" A shy smile ghosted around her mouth.

Cindy sat up straight. "No, I haven't had time. Why?"

Mildred grinned.

"Mil! Did he comment again? What did he say?" Cindy groped around in her purse for her phone and pulled up the account as fast as she could.

"Look under the announcement for The Gardens."

Cindy scrolled down, then squealed in delight. "What's this Moonflower stuff?"

Mildred shrugged, blushing. "It's what he calls me."

"Really? Moonflower? How utterly romantic. And, fluff the pillows? Really? Is that some kind of code for you-know-what?"

Mildred swatted at her friend, not taking eyes off the road. "Just trying to be hospitable."

"Mil, do you realize he's liked every post you've made since we met him at Mountain Stage? And most of them are flowers and dirt and growing stuff. What traveling music man cares about that? And every time your face is in the shot? He comments. Every. Single. Time."

Mildred lifted her hand up to her mouth and tried to stop her grin from spreading. But it was no use. She couldn't stop smiling. "It's all in fun, C. Just pretend stuff. You know how I feel about romantic gobbledy goop. We will never, ever see each other again.

Besides, I think he still has that girlfriend. That Heather-what's-her-face. The one who sang backups on his first album."

"Oh, phoo! Forget about her. I thought they were history. I bet he doesn't comment on *her* Instagram."

"I don't think she uses hers much." A rosy blush spread over Mildred's cheeks.

"Stalking?"

"Well, I was just curious. Gil doesn't have a lot of followers. His account is private. When I saw Heather on his list, I just clicked over. She only has, like, two posts. And they're from months ago. She doesn't do Facebook, either. As long as I'm confessing."

Cindy side-eyed Mildred. "Well, it doesn't matter. No sense overanalyzing it. Just enjoy the banter. It's about time you let someone catch your eye. Even if it *is* only on Instagram. Fifteen years is too long, Mil. Time to forget the past and start fresh. How many West Virginia girls can say they have a flirtation with a music star? Might as well have fun with it."

Mildred was quiet for a moment, letting her eyes follow the road. Then: "Fifteen years. Has it really been that long?" She studied the road in front of her. "You know what? You're right. Might as well have fun. I've got nothing to lose, do I?"

She pulled into the church lot, swerved lopsided into a parking spot and shifted the truck into park. They came to a jolting stop. Mildred rested her hands on the wheel a second. Then she turned to Cindy and said, "Let's go hear about refugees."

~

Neither of them spoke on the way home. The steady hum of the road rolling beneath them filled the quiet. The moon was on the wane but still flooded the hills with hopeful light. Mildred pulled into the drive and up beside the barn. She shifted into park and turned off the ignition. Neither she nor Cindy moved.

Staring straight ahead at the moon-bathed hills surrounding The Gardens, Mildred said, "We have to do something, Cindy."

"I know, Mildred. I know."

"I'm calling the Refugee Resettlement Services tomorrow."

"Okay, Mildred."

Mildred glanced sidelong at Cindy. "Will you help me do this?"

Cindy sighed and unbuckled her seatbelt. "We've been best friends since we were five years old, Mil. Every major thing that's happened in my life, you were with me. The backpacking trip after high school. My wedding day." She paused. "When we buried Shelby. The day I filed for divorce. But not just the hard stuff, the good stuff too. There's no way I'd ever have had the courage to start something like The Gardens if you weren't doing it with me. Whatever you do, Mil, I'm always going to do it with you. As long as you want me to."

"I'll always want you to, Cindy. You've always been there for me too. I never could have made it—fifteen years ago—without you. You're my sister, you know that?" Mildred's voice caught and she felt her eyes begin to well.

"Oh, stop," Cindy teased. "For a tomboy you always cried too easily. Give me a hug." They both giggled, and Mildred awkwardly leaned over for a quick embrace.

And because her heart was still tender from thinking about fifteen years ago, Mildred said, as they climbed out of the truck, "You know, C, we make a pretty good team. Who needs a man around anyway?"

~

"Cindy!" Mildred kicked off her clogs at the door and dropped the umbrella on the boot tray. She peeled off her rain jacket and draped it over the high-backed chair in the entry.

"I'm in here." Cindy's muted voice sang through the heavy kitchen door. Mildred burst in to find Cindy alone, puzzling over a plate of walnut chocolate chip cookies. "There's something missing," she said, as she took a noiseless bite.

"Just a minute," Mildred said. She went to the fridge and pulled out a glass jar of milk. Reaching for two juice glasses from the open-air cupboard, she set them on the counter and poured. She put one glass down in front of Cindy and grabbed a cookie for herself. They both took a bite simultaneously and washed it down with a swig of milk.

"Perfect!" they said, in unison, then laughed at the shared timing.

Cindy put her glass down. "Is it still raining?"

"Yes, sheets. But it's all good. The flowers we planted last week need a good drink. This saves me the trouble."

"Mmm." Cindy stretched. "But this weather makes me sleepy. Is it nap time yet?"

"I have news."

Cindy turned a steady gaze on Mildred.

"Okay?"

"Guess where I've been all morning?"

"I wouldn't even try," Cindy said, dryly.

"We-ell. I got up early."

"You usually do."

"And I called Valisha at the Charities Organization."

"And what did you and Valisha talk about?"

"We-ell... I got so excited during our conversation that she convinced me I should come to the office straight away..."

"She convinced you, eh?"

"You know what I mean."

"I'm sure I do."

"Anyway, C, take a look at this!"

She pulled a brightly colored file, red with black polka dots, out of her bag and lay it on the table in front of Cindy with a flourish. Cindy looked at the file with one eyebrow raised.

"Go ahead! Open it."

Cindy flipped open the folder to the first page. A family of four smiled up at her from a glossy photo. A youngish, handsome couple and their two cinnamon-skinned daughters. The family was so beautiful that Cindy's breath caught.

"Mil? Is this just a promo picture? This isn't the family you're considering to sponsor?"

"We're sponsoring. Not just me. And yes, this is the Agha family: the dad's name is Deza, the mom is Delal, the girls are Lelia and Vian. Vian is eight. Lelia, twelve. Turn the page, Cindy. You have to read their story."

Cindy studied the faces of the Agha family. She touched Vian's face with a finger. "They're just so... so... beautiful."

"I know, right? I just, well, after listening to Zahura, I asked Valisha if there was a family with daughters who might be interested in coming here. I can't stand the thought of any more girls stuck..."

"Where is this family right now?"

"What?"

"Are they safe? Where do they stay until we get them here?"

"Most refugees stay in displaced persons camps until they're found a better place."

"Displaced persons camps? I don't like the sound of that."

Mildred studied Cindy's flushed face. A smile slowly spread across hers.

"Cindy."

"What?"

"Read the rest of the file. You're not going to believe it."

Cindy picked up the file and left the kitchen for her favorite comfy chair in the sunroom. Mildred followed her, carrying her milk and another cookie. Pete followed Mildred. They sat beneath the music of rain pattering on the glass panels, Mildred stroking Petey's soft fur while Cindy read.

Ten minutes later, Cindy looked up. "Are you kidding me?"

"I know, right?"

"Deza is a gardener? And Delal is a cook? Mildred, they're perfect!" Cindy resumed scanning the documents. "Listen to this, 'I can make anything grow,' says Deza, flashing a brilliant smile. 'The terrain of my homeland is most inhospitable, but I made my community beautiful with my hands and with my heart for growing things.'" She looked up again and her eyes were misty. Mildred put a hand on Cindy's arm.

"I was thinking we could clean out Uncle Van's old house on the far south part of the property. It's been empty for ten years. But it's a sweet little house. Two big bedrooms. And Van's office could be turned into a small one if they ever wanted. The living room and kitchen are open and airy, and the screened porch he built the year before he had his stroke is lovely. The road that goes out there might need some attention, but it runs right behind The Glasshouse, so Deza could walk over there to work the flowers every morning. I don't know, I just…when I read their bios it just seemed like it was meant to be."

"It does seem that way, doesn't it?" Cindy held Mildred's gaze. "Honestly? I wasn't sure at first. We have…so much on our hands with the opening and all. But now it seems too good to be true. I've been overwhelmed at everything that's going to go into running the kitchen, Mil. I mean, if all I had to do was cook, that'd be one thing. But manage staff? All the health department crap? And the math. There's so much math. And this says three generations of Delal's family have been the cooks for the village special events. I don't know if she can help with all the logistical stuff, but she might. It's like a gift. And with all the trouble you're having getting Jim to listen to you? A gardener for Pete's sake!"

Petey's ears twitched at the mention of his name.

"For Pete's sake," Mildred repeated, into the thick fur on the dog's neck. Pete turned and licked the air around her face. Mildred dodged his tongue.

"Of course, they have to agree to come here first. And work for us for the modest pay we can afford right now. I hope over time it will get better. But a couple like this—with such skills— they may have some other choices. I don't know how that works. I do know that one of the strikes against us is the lack of other Yezidi people here. Charleston has about twenty right now, Valisha says that's only four families. In our favor is the fact that one of those families is Delal's brother and his people. But there's a larger community of Yezidis in Lincoln, Nebraska, and a lot of Yezidis start out somewhere else but eventually end up in Nebraska. The resettlement services have targeted this area as another with a lot of potential, and they are trying to encourage families to come here with good learning opportunities. They have the beginnings of a culture center here—a place for refugees to learn English and basic life skills like money management and stuff. They're modeling Charleston's services after the one in Lincoln because it's been so successful. There are over 3,000 Yezidi people there."

"Nebraska?" Cindy's voice was incredulous. "Mildred, we have to get on this. What if they go to Nebraska? What if someone else snaps them up? I feel it in my spirit this family is supposed to be here with us."

Mildred laughed in delight. "I'm glad to hear you're so keen. I filled out the paperwork this morning. Father Mike has a team of guys coming over tomorrow to help me move some of the old stuff out of Uncle Van's cottage. I'm planning a video for our Instagram to solicit donations. If everything goes as it should, the Agha family will be here this time next month." She paused briefly, remembering the morning. "Cindy?"

"Um-hmm?" Cindy said, still studying the portfolio.

"When we were talking this morning, Valisha said something about sponsoring the Aghas that I can't stop thinking about."

Cindy looked up. "What's that?"

"She said, 'You are going to be their anchor in the sea of this new beginning. So you must be strong because your life will never be the same again either.'"

Cindy blinked and looked down at the four faces staring up at her from the glossy photo.

"I'm sure she is very right about that."

~

"They're coming!" Mildred left her phone on the library desk and jogged downstairs. She burst through the kitchen door.

"They're coming! I just got off the phone with Valisha. The Aghas accepted our invitation to live and work here!"

Cindy closed her iPad quickly and beamed at Mildred. "That's awesome!"

Mildred skipped around the table and grabbed both of Cindy's hands. She skip-jumped in a circle, taking Cindy with her.

"I'm so excited, C! I can't believe we're going to get to do this! Valisha says this is significant in helping to build a new community for the Yezidi people. It feels so good to have a safe place for them. For their girls."

Cindy giggled at Mildred's exuberance. "When will they come? What do we need to do? I have a million questions!"

"The main thing we need to focus on is getting Uncle Van's house ready for them. There's a protocol Valisha will follow to help them adjust to the community—you know, English classes and culture stuff—so we can focus on being their new family. Let's walk down to Uncle Van's and see where we need to start. The guys hauled away a lot of junk last week. It's going to need a good scrubbing."

Cindy hesitated. She picked up her iPad up and fiddled with the case. "This is huge, Mil," she said, setting the iPad in front of Mildred and opening the cover. "I don't want to put a damper on things. But there's something I want you to see before we head over to Uncle Van's."

She tapped in her security code and closed out the recipe box that popped up, then pulled up another page, turning the screen to face Mildred. Mildred looked at the screen before her and then at Cindy questioningly.

"Yes?"

Cindy hit play and a news report started rolling.

"Our sources at Nashville General Hospital tell us that long-time girlfriend of singer-songwriter Sam Gillenwater was treated for a heroin overdose last week," a twenty-something hipster with a full beard was saying into the camera.

"Oh, no!" Mildred turned up the volume.

"Heather Watts was admitted through the ER late Sunday morning. Our sources say Sam Gillenwater did not leave her bedside her entire stay."

A video clip of an exhausted-looking Sam popped up, his back to a hospital room door and reporters barraging him with questions. Mildred's heart ached at the tired, bewildered expression on his face. His dark hair was tousled and it looked like he hadn't shaved in days.

The clip disappeared and the hipster was sitting at a desk. "Sam Gillenwater has been very vocal about his anti-drug stance since Watts' first overdose last Christmas. The camera-shy singer-songwriter usually manages to stay out of the limelight, but with the smash success of his latest album, *Oddbird*, and its accompanying rigorous tour, he's been in the public eye more than usual. This, however, is not the kind of publicity a rumored grammy nominee needs right now. We caught up with Gillenwater's manager, Scott Chambers."

The clip showed a wiry man in a suit walking briskly up a street. A reporter clamored along beside him. "Mr. Chambers, what do you have to say about Heather Watts' drug overdose?" She shoved a mic in his face.

He didn't look into the camera or attempt to speak in the mic. "Heather Watts is a dear, dear friend of my client, Sam Gillenwater. Ms. Watts is recovering from this unfortunate incident and is seeking professional help. End of statement."

"Mr. Chambers, we're told that Gil was with Heather when she overdosed. Mr. Chambers, does your client use drugs? Was he doing heroin with Heather when this happened?"

Scott stopped abruptly and looked squarely into the camera, cheeks reddening. "Let me make this clear, and I'm only going to say this once. Sam Gillenwater does not use drugs. He never has. He hates the stuff. It has broken his heart to watch some of his closest friends fall prey to addiction. He has been with Heather as she recovers—hasn't left her side—because that is the kind of friend he is. End of story."

He pushed the camera away and trudged off.

The hipster reappeared on the screen. "There you have it folks. Truth? Or fiction? Time has a way of revealing the story."

Cindy reached over and closed out the screen. "That's pretty much it. They talk about her last overdose, how it was prescription pills that time. Speculate about Gil's role in the thing— did he break up with her? Why was she at his house? But it's all just sensational bullshit. The real story is the look on his face when those reporters show up at the hospital. Here's a guy who almost lost a good friend and you're going to do what? Ambush him?"

Mildred was quiet. She kept replaying that image over and over in her mind. The broken look on his face. Fear. "I feel so bad for him. It must have been awful."

"I know. He looked a bit like a deer in headlights. I think you should message him."

Mildred looked up. "Message him? I can't do that! He'll think I'm just listening to gossip. This is his private life. I don't want to be creepy."

"Well, are you friends or not? Seems to me like you guys have some kind of connection, or something. The creepy thing would be to not acknowledge someone he cares about almost died."

Mildred looked back down at the screen. "I don't know. I need to think."

Cindy tossed her a duster from the counter. "You can think while we clean. Let's get up to Van's and check it out."

Mildred caught the duster and studied it for a minute. Then she remembered. She looked up at Cindy. "Well, I've nothing to lose, do I?"

KAY NGUYEN

[june-july]

"Your body was born of stardust." She heard a psychologist say this on TV last week. He was talking about the beginning of time, when the stars exploded. "Most of the molecules that make up your body were created inside a star," he said. Wren was bringing noodles to her as she watched TV, reclined on the couch. "Why do you cry, Mom?" she had asked, alarmed. Her daughter left the noodles on the lamp table and knelt in front of her, placed smooth hands upon her sagging shoulders and pressed her forehead to Kay's. Wren's eyes opened and closed, blinking back her own tears. "We still have time, Mom. We will make this time beautiful."

Kay couldn't answer, lost in the thought of starlight glowing inside her. *What was wrong with the stars that birthed my bones?* she wondered. *Why has my life been the story of sorrow?* But she didn't voice these questions. No good would come of it. She patted Wren's cheek and gave her a weak smile. "I know. I know, my daughter." They ate the noodles together in silence, listening to the doctor describe the birth of the world from starfire.

Today, she was looking out the window and wondering, *how do we make this time beautiful?*

The hillside they lived on was falling. In the dim light of the coming dawn Kay noticed a pile of stone debris just 200 yards from their property line. Larger stones surrounded by smaller rocks and dirt. Their newest neighbor did not consider shifting earth when he built his house so far up the incline two years ago. So many contractors brought in over these past months to help figure out how to keep his million-dollar home from sliding down the hill. Kay looked at the pile of rubble. This was how she felt: her body in a slow downhill glide. *What must it feel like to come to the bottom? Would it be a slow, rolling stop? Or a sudden crash?*

She was dying. Not today, not tomorrow—maybe not for some time, no one would say. But this much she knew: no treatment could eradicate the cancer creeping along her bones now, spreading out, clinging to her spinal column and twining into her lungs and other unseen places. Get your affairs in order, they said. Spend time with those you love, they said. Make the most of the time you are given.

She shook her head and tried to think of *beautiful* again.

The summer storms these past few days had left everything waterlogged and droopy. She could see the air heavy with moisture in the way her bedroom window collected the dew. Queen Anne's Lace in the empty lot beside them spoke the memory of rain. The day was beginning with thousands of drops of light, dripping from leaf and bole. The grass was littered with yellow leaves from the walnut tree, tiny boats sailing the wet land. She watched a baby rabbit disappear through a door of bending grasses.

The coming of morning brought a clarity she hadn't felt in weeks. She lifted herself up with some effort and moved closer to the window pane. She leaned her forehead against the glass, watched as a slow-moving cloud glided over the rosy horizon. Her breath was vapor, condensing on the cool glass. She pressed her thumb in the middle of that beading bit of moisture.

I can touch this misty life. As sure as breath moving in and out of me, the vapor of it leaves a residue on my fingers. I leave fingerprints on this world.

So many days lately she'd been sleepwalking through the minutes. Hazy with pain or medication. Missing the beauty right here, before her eyes, on this tiny plot of land on which she and her husband chose to begin their life together. Back when the property was not so costly. When the closest neighbor was three miles away. So many years ago. So many things had changed since she was a young bride with rosy cheeks and eyes filled with starlight. How long had Raymond been gone now? Twenty-eight years. Died much too young, and tragically. She was left to raise Wren alone, with no family, no friends, to help. The settlement from the factory allowed them time to grieve and also the funds to open the restaurant—a long awaited dream. What else could she do? She had no skills except to cook. The memories of her mother's kitchen in Saigon, imprinted on her heart and mind, burned their way through her hands and fingertips, until all she could do was cook. Cook and remember.

It was strange, as she drew closer to death, that thoughts of Raymond did not haunt. Rather, it was *Thia* she kept returning to. She closed her eyes and saw her sister's face as clear as when she was a girl. The brightness in the older girl's eyes never faded. Thia, the beautiful one. Perhaps it was her beauty that killed her in the end.

Though Kay's family regularly attended the Catholic church in the square, she also kept some of the old ways. She kept the family altar and offered prayers for her ancestors. Sometimes, when she knelt with her candle, she felt Thia smiling on her.

"I pray I see you soon, dear sister," she whispered into the glass. Kay heard Wren stirring in the kitchen, smelled the dark coffee her daughter favored as it began to brew. She backed away from the window and sat back down in her chair. She heard Wren's small feet pad quietly down the hall and pause outside her door. The knob turned and Wren's furrowed brow appeared.

"Mom? Are you awake?"

Kay shifted her gaze to her daughter's worried face.

"I am."

Wren entered the room and sat down on the edge of her mother's bed.

"What would you like for breakfast today? I found some beautiful peaches at market yesterday. I can slice those up and put some on oatmeal. Or, there's still yogurt and eggs in the fridge."

Kay sighed. Always with the food. Her daughter thought feeding her would somehow make her well.

"Don't worry about that. I'll make myself something in a bit."

"Mom."

"I promise, Wren! Don't bother yourself so. Shouldn't you be at the restaurant?"

"I'm covered."

"Who's covering for you, that husband of yours?"

"Yes."

"Who has the boys?"

"The boys are with Cal. He's just supervising the kitchen staff. It's all under control. Don't worry, Mother." She rose from the bed and bent to kiss the top of Kay's head.

"Will you at least join me in the kitchen for coffee? There's something I need to show you."

Kay looked at her daughter absently. "Something to show me? You are so mysterious." There was little of this world, besides her grandsons, that she cared to see these days. Wren knew this. Yet Kay rose from her chair anyway. "Just let me get my housecoat."

Wren had the robe in hand. When did she become so quick? Kay threaded her arms through the offered sleeves. They ambled to the kitchen, Wren following her closely with arms out—as if her tiny frame could catch her if she wobbled. Kay settled into one of the chairs in the breakfast nook. Wren poured two mugs of coffee—black—and joined her mom.

Kay could see the girl was fretting over something. What could possibly cause worry at this point?

"What is it then, Wren? What do you want to show me?"

Wren hesitated, then got up from the table and retrieved her iPad from her tote. She propped it in front of her mother and tapped the screen a few times. Kay watched her daughter's face as she made ready whatever this was. There was a hint of a smile at the corner of Wren's mouth, but also worry on her brow. Kay felt the first tiny bit of curiosity. She shifted in the chair and focused on the screen.

It was some kind of press conference. A young man was standing at a podium as reporters shuffled in around him. Finally, the room quieted and the man cleared his throat.

"For those of you who do not know me, my name is Sam Gillenwater. Most of you probably know me by 'Gil.' Maybe some of you have heard that my latest album, *Oddbird,* was mentioned in *Nashville Sound* last week as a probable nomination for a Grammy."

Kay looked up at Wren with her eyebrows raised.

"Keep watching," her daughter said.

He was a musician, this Sam Gillenwater. But why should she care? Kay could not fathom what her daughter was up to. Still, Wren was intent on the screen so Kay kept her eyes on it too.

The man called Sam lifted his eyes and paused. He blinked. Something in his face looked familiar. Kay leaned closer. "Earlier this year I almost lost someone I care about, and it changed something in me. I can't explain it except to say that I'm realizing how fragile life can be, how little time we have, and I want my time to make a difference. Something beyond the music."

On the screen behind him an image of a newspaper article from 1979 appeared. The USS Edwin Phillips Rescues 438 Vietnamese Boat People," the headline read. Another article flashed. "Infant Born on Vietnamese Refugee Boat, Mother Dies."

Kay froze.

"Some of you may know I was adopted as an infant." A murmur traveled through the room.

Kay's heart was pounding out of her chest. "Wren?"

"Keep watching," her daughter said, eyes glistening. She reached over and took her mother's hand. The man called Sam kept speaking—about the rescue, the pirates, the infant boy.

Kay put a hand to her mouth and stood up. She thought she might pass out. She looked at Wren as tears spilled from her eyes.

"It can't be…"

Wren reached over and hit 'pause.'

"It is, mother. Sam Gillenwater is my cousin. Your nephew. The child of your sister Thia."

Kay dropped back down into the chair. "How? Where did you find this? When…?"

She didn't know what to say. She studied the face on the

screen. "Can you zoom in? I want to see him."

Wren zoomed in on Sam's face. "Do you want to hear the rest?"

Kay couldn't take her eyes off him. There was her sister's nose. Her mouth. The shape of her jaw. "Yes, yes."

Kay watched, rapt. *This is my nephew,* she kept thinking. At the end, Wren silently closed the iPad. Kay was motionless but her entire body was shaking. She couldn't control the sobs wracking her being from the inside out. Wren put her arms around her mother.

"Mother?"

"Does he know, Wren? Does he know about us?"

"Yes. And he wants to meet us. He's coming to California next week. He has several shows to do, but he has carved out time for us. Can you handle this, Mom? I was so afraid to tell you."

"Yes, Wren. I can handle this. I *must* handle this." She turned her tear-streaked face to her daughter. "After all these years. I didn't even know if he was still alive! Please. Please, daughter. Tell me everything you know."

~

He came on Thursday, senior day at the restaurant. Kay wore her best dress and waited for him at a quiet table in the back room. It was her favorite place to meet when talking was important—the floor-to-ceiling glass windows overlooking the adjacent park made for a pleasant backdrop. It was too hot for her on the patio. This way they would be treated to occasional glimpses of the horseback riders on the trail that wound around the valley.

Wren sat beside her mother, white-knuckled and pinch-faced. Kay knew her daughter worried that the excitement would be too much for her. And she had been a bit beside herself, unable to stop the trembling inside. She had spoken to Sam on the phone, but they agreed to wait to ask all the questions filling their hearts. She knew he wanted to know of his mother. All morning her thoughts had turned to Thia. What to tell the boy? There was so much. And again, she found herself in tears as she tried to organize a lifetime of sorrow and love in her mind. Wren reached over and took her hand.

They were sitting like this when Sam came. He took off his hat when he saw her, lifted it to his heart and stood, frozen, in the middle of the room. A man in a tan suit was filming with his iPhone, and a thin woman stood beside him with a camera around her neck. A woman with red hair clutched Sam's arm. Kay saw her give his hand a squeeze. *This must be the sister,* she thought. The one he called Sher.

For an endless moment, time seemed to stand still as they took each other in. He was taller than she thought he'd be—this, from his father, of course. But his face! How could he look so American and yet still so like Thia?

Wren stood to meet him, and he clasped her hands in both of his. "How will I ever be able to thank you enough?" he asked, in a hoarse whisper. Wren felt a wave of warmth wash over her. This man was her cousin! She started to say something but Kay lifted out of her seat, and Sam, seeing her struggle, hurried to the table. "No, please, don't get up." He sat beside her. Sher followed and the two filming quickly shuffled behind them, leaning in and out to, presumably, capture the best angle. Sam turned in his seat, annoyed. "That's enough, Scott. I said only a few shots when we first meet."

"But we will do some more formal shots after you talk, right Gil? We talked about this."

Sam gave an exasperated sigh. "I guess so, Scotty, but come on! A little space? Please."

Scotty pulled a small digital recorder out of his pocket and pointed from it to the table. "Okay?" he said, as he leaned over and put the device between Sam and Kay. He tapped a button to get the device going. Sam rolled his eyes and looked apologetically at Kay. "I'm so sorry about all this."

Kay had not taken her eyes off him since he sat down. Her eyes welled with tears. "I cannot believe it is you," she whispered.

He smiled weakly. "And I cannot believe it is you."

They both chuckled.

"I held you. When you were born. We've seen each other before." She smiled, caught her breath when she noticed his eyes. "There is so much to say. I don't know where to begin."

"I feel the same way."

Kay looked at Sher and back to Sam. "It seems you have made a good life, despite your difficult beginning. This makes me happy. And I know it would make Thia happy too."

He seemed to be caught by the mention of his mother's name, but then he smiled. "Yes. I had a good childhood. I have been loved well." He glanced to his side. "This is my sister, Sher, who I told you about."

Kay held clasped Sher's hands in hers. "Welcome, Sher,"

Sher smiled, but made no comment.

The man in the tan suit coughed and Sam startled, as if he'd forgotten his presence.

"Oh, yes, and this is my publicist, Scotty Chambers and our social media director April Billings." Sam dipped his head apologetically. "Scott and April will release some of this footage on the website, as I explained to you on the phone. I'm sorry. Scotty thinks," he caught himself. "We—think telling part of this story might help publicize our refugee tour and bring more support to the cause. I've made him promise not to overdo it ..."

Kay smiled with her whole face. "I understand completely. This is part of your life. Wren showed me your press conference. You are a superstar! As long as I can have you to myself for a little while, I don't mind sharing you with your fans."

Sam laughed and lowered his eyes. "Thank you..." he hesitated. "I don't know what to call you. Should I say 'Aunt'? Or 'Kay'? 'Auntie'?" He laughed nervously. "What do you think? My parents were both only children so I have no other reference point. You are my only aunt."

Kay felt her face flush with pleasure. "To be called 'Auntie' would be...sweet? If you like, and if it feels right, you may call me Dì, which is the term we would use for your mother's younger sister in Vietnamese."

Sam considered. "How about if I call you Dì Kay?"

Kay smiled. "Perfect."

Everyone smiled and shifted in their seats uncomfortably. Sam spoke again.

"Dì Kay, is it hard for you to speak of the way you left your country? Will you tell me your story? Will you tell me *my* story?"

Kay swallowed. "I have pondered this since we first spoke. I think...we must go back—farther. We will begin with the day our lives changed forever. Wren, will you bring some water? And maybe some dumplings. This will take some time."

She closed her eyes and let her breathing slow, peeling back the years with her mind until she was younger—much younger: a skinny girl with no breasts standing barefoot in front of a yellow door tipping back and forth in the breeze.

~

"In the autumn of my tenth year my father was taken to the Long Thanh reeducation camp."

She hesitated.

"I don't know how much you know about this part of our history. The 'camps' were glorified prisons set up by the government to punish my people for their alliance with the United States during the war. The public aim was to 'rehabilitate' offenders to make them acceptable members of Communist society. But the English word 'reeducate' doesn't quite explain the intention of the camps the way the original language does: *trại học tập cải tạo*. *Tạo* means *to create* and Cải, *to transform*. The purpose of the camps was to create new people. To destroy any remaining traces of the old ways. And destroy the spirits of the people who lived them out.

I was so young—I didn't understand. I knew Ba was a soldier for the ARVN, and that some of his work was secret, for there were always people coming and going from our house in the night. I did not know he was a high-ranking intelligence officer, a chief strategist for our army. I only knew that he was my Ba and he was doing important work for our country.

It was September of 1975, when they came—just months after the fall of Saigon.

When they took him, we thought it would only be for a short time. He was told a week to ten days. I remember how we all lined up outside our house and gave him honor as we said our goodbyes. I remember the dark eyes of the officers who escorted him away from us—how they lingered on my sister longer than necessary. Thia was 15, and her beauty was only beginning to flower. But already she attracted long stares wherever we went. She was an innocent, protected by my father's status and our faith. But Thia was not naïve. The war did not allow us that luxury. I saw fear in her eyes that day.

My father showed no fear. He held his head high as he greeted each of us. I, being the least, was last in line to say good-bye. When Ba knelt down to me, he looked into my eyes for the longest time—I had the sense he was trying to memorize my face. The intensity of his gaze frightened me some, and I began to cry. He cupped my cheek and pressed his forehead to mine and told me that I must be brave. *Your mother and your sister will need you,* he said to me.

One of the officers nudged him with his rifle. They ushered him into a military vehicle. He did not look back at us as they pulled away. Only forward. We never saw him again."

Kay paused in her telling and took a drink of water. Sam reached over and squeezed her hand. She looked up at him with a sad smile.

"It's okay, *con nhỏ của tôi*—*my little one*. Unfortunately, our story is not uncommon among my people. We shared in so much suffering. So much grief. No one remained untouched by loss. We were fortunate to have others walk through the sorrow with us. This sharing of the pain makes the burden less heavy."

She took a deep breath, eyes shining, and continued.

"As soon as the car carrying Ba away disappeared behind the hopea trees that lined our street, Ma sprang into action. Someone would return for us. We all knew this. Especially for my sister, someone would return. In secret, my Ma and Ba had planned for this day. Ma had packed travel bags for us. She cut off all of Thia's hair and burned it in the back yard. Ba had arranged through some of his old alliances for our safe passage through the city. Ma dressed me and my sister as boys and schooled us in what to say should we be questioned. My brother and I were going to the country to work on my uncle's rice farm. Our mother would cook for him, as his wife went to sleep with our ancestors a few weeks ago. We have been merchants in the city—no political ties or opinions—but our uncle needs us now. Our father had disappeared many years gone. We were alone in the world, making our way as best as we could. We were invisible. Nobodies. Nothing. This was the only way to stay safe. To stay safe from the officers' dark eyes.

We were taken to a safe place. To go to our real family would put them in danger. It was best we disappeared. We were hidden deep in the jungle on a farm compound of ARVN soldiers' families, all living together as one. We had a new story, a new history, a new name. Together we would create a new reality.

It did work, for a time. We were as happy at the farm as we could have been anywhere else. But, without Ba, happy moments fell flat. Laughter rang hollow and echoed into another time, another place. Ma tried many times but was unable to find word about Ba. She went to Long Thanh on family day, but Ba was not there. One of the things the reeducation camps did was relocate the prisoners periodically, making it difficult for families to keep track of their loved ones. No one could, or would, tell her where he'd gone. Only that he was moved to a work camp. We heard terrible stories of cruelty, disease and starvation.

Ma stopped eating. She began to wither away before our eyes. Thia and I were her only reasons to remain alive.

One year passed. Two. In the third year we were discovered by some government officials. They carefully recorded our information and left us alone for a few months. But they returned after the spring crop. Most of the men were taken. The women and children were allowed to stay, for a time. The officers took most of our food supply as well. Leaving us with few stores for the coming monsoon season. We sent word to Ma's brother, Uncle Binh. He sent my eldest cousin, Thu and his sister, Tam, for us. Uncle believed we would be safe to resume our real identities. He was in good standing with the government—a tobacco farmer. We traveled for two days, by foot and cart. I will never forget the hardship of that journey. Ma was so tired. I was afraid we would lose her. But my cousin was kind and he insisted she ride in the cart for most of the way.

Uncle Binh's farm was small, but busy. He used to brag that if he had more workers he could produce twice the crop. We all went to work immediately and learned every job so that we could fill in where needed. It was difficult work. And many became ill with the green tobacco sickness. We did not know about such things then. We did not know to wear gloves and handle to leaves with care. Thia became very ill and so was taken out of the fields. She helped Ma and my aunt in the kitchen, feeding the workers and the family. Gradually, she regained her health but she never seemed to completely regain her strength.

One day, an American came to us through the trees. This was concerning—the Americans had been gone for some time. We had almost forgotten the paleness of their skin, the rounded curve of their eyes. His name was Stephen, but we called him

Bầu trời, which is Vietnamese for *sky*, for his eyes were the same blue as that of the heavens. Kay paused and looked intensely into Sam's face for a minute. Then she looked out the window with a furrowed brow, like she was trying to remember something.

"Dì Kay?"

"Sky was a journalist documenting the aftermath of the war on our people. That was what he told us. He was a former soldier who had returned to America disillusioned and saddened by what he left behind in Vietnam. He decided to come back to us, to step back into the place that had been hell to him and try to find a way to redemption. He lived, as they say, undercover. In hiding. He was doing a story on the reeducation camps and had been to the compound we had just left. He asked for us by name, telling the women who were still there he had a message from Ba. They told him how to find us. He put himself in much danger to trace our steps.

I do not know the entire story and many details have died from the passage of time. But Sky told my mother he had come upon a band of escapees from one of the camps as he traveled in secret. This band was led by Ba. Fate sometimes enjoys giving gifts, it seems. Sky and Ba had fought side-by-side in the war. They knew each other well and Ba vouched for his character to the others. They welcomed him into their group as a fellow outcast. Ba was interested in Sky's work, this shedding of light on truth. They had many conversations about politics and life. My Ba loved to talk about such things. He was...very...*rich?* in mind and enjoyed ideas. Sky was the same way. They became close confidantes. Ba told Sky about his family. How he wanted to come to us. But there was unrest with Cambodia and he did not trust the safety of it. He feared if he returned to us he would lead death to our door. He made Sky promise to find us if anything happened to him." Dì Kay paused then quietly said, "Sky kept his promise."

Sam, who had clung to every word, dropped his head. "I'm sorry." He looked up and held his aunt's eyes. "Your father. My grandfather." The word felt strange on his tongue. "How?"

Kay wiped a tear from her cheek and shrugged weakly.

"Ma would not allow anyone to tell us the details. We only knew that it was by the hand of the government that our father was killed. Sky insisted that, in his death, Ba saved the lives of several men, including his own. It was late February in 1978. Almost two and a half years since our father was taken from us. Life had been hard, but until this news we still had hope. A world without Ba was a world without hope. Our lives were no longer recognizable to us.

Sky stayed with us for two weeks. One morning we woke up and he was gone."

Sam felt a sinking feeling at these words. Disappointment. And fear began to niggle at the back of his mind.

"We were all sad. We liked the American. He was our last link to Ba. But we knew he would be putting himself—and us— in danger to linger.

The news of Ba's death sent Ma into despair. She took to her bed. Thia and I took turns feeding her, sitting with her, singing to her. We tried to prepare our hearts for her to leave us. We had almost given up. She had given up. Then Sky returned."

Kay glanced at Sam for his reaction. She was rewarded when a light rekindled in his eyes.

"He had been shot through his right shoulder and lost a lot of blood. The wound was growing infection and by the time he made his way back to us he was delirious with fever. Sky's desperate need awakened Ma from her sleep. She, with Thia's help, nursed him as a mother would her child. Every day I was in the field, doing my work for Uncle. In the evening, after dinner, I was to give Thia a break from her nursing duties. But she would never leave. She sat with a basin of cool water and continually washed the heat of his fever away. Slowly, he came back to us.

By the time he was well enough to walk short distances around the farm, Thia had fallen in love with Sky. It's not difficult to understand how this happened. We all had fallen in love with him a little by then. He had a poet's heart. Even in delirium his way of seeing pointed us back to the beauty still alive in the world. He had seen terrible things, as we all had. Death and hatred and destruction. Yet, Sky's belief in justice and goodness would not allow him to turn away from all the ugliness of war—of what war left behind. And still he saw the good. Not only this, but he gave us back our mother. He was wise enough to understand that grief sometimes requires a midwife. He let himself be that for Ma. He refused to eat unless she did also. He asked for her help in walking, giving her a reason to move, as he leaned into her and she leaned into him. We all could see what he was doing. I loved him for it too. But Thia..."

Kay shook her head. "How could we know? How could we not know? She spent every waking hour with him. She had bathed him and dressed him and fed him like a babe. I saw the tender way they looked at each other. But in our culture, good girls did not..."

She paused again, at a loss for words and lifted both her hands in question.

"But love makes its own rules. There was no inkling of suspicion they had been intimate. Love, yes, but the other? We did not know. Not until he had been gone for months. Not until Thia's belly began to swell."

Sam let this sink in. His mind was racing. Kay looked into her nephew's face again.

"Yes," she said, finally. "You have his eyes, my nephew."

Her words were like a sucker punch and all of Sam's breath was gone. "My father?" He whispered, feeling the blood drain from his face. "Sky is my father?"

Kay smiled and held Sam's eyes with her own. "Yes. He was a good man."

Sam felt something unwind inside him. He hadn't realized how afraid he had been. Too afraid to hope he had been conceived in love. So many possibilities about his father stirred in his mind as Dì Kay told her story. The sense of relief made his eyes sting.

"It is a lot for you to take in, I know. But know that you were made in love. By two people caught in terrible circumstances. If things had been different...a different time...I don't know. But you are here. We are here together. For this, I am grateful."

"But, what happened, Dì Kay? What happened to my father?"

Kay sighed. "I do not know the end of his story, Sam dear. As soon as Sky knew Ma would be okay, he started making plans to leave the country. The bullet that injured him had shattered his right shoulder. We sewed a sling for him to keep his shoulder in place, but he remained in constant pain. He knew he would need a delicate surgery if ever he would be able to use his arm again. A surgery he could not pursue in hiding in Vietnam. Things happened quickly. He had contacts in the military and in the American government. A rendezvous was arranged. I do know that he asked Thia to go with him. I heard them, through the door the night before he disappeared. He wanted her to leave with him. But he could not take all three of us. And she would not leave us. They argued into silence. Through the door, I heard them weeping together. The next morning, he was gone."

Sam waited.

"I wish I could tell you more," Kay said, apologetically. "I don't know if your father made it back to America. I don't even know his real name."

"What do you mean, 'his real name?'"

Kay shrugged and shook her head.

"This may sound crazy but after he left, we wondered if Sky may have been more than what he told us. When I came of age, I began to ask many questions. Questions I was too young and too afraid to ask when I first came to this country. Through much determination and legwork, I was able to find out more about Stephen. In the eighties, there were a few reunions of some of the veterans who fought in the war who had made it to the United States. It was a way to try to make sense of what they'd been through. At first, I went as a way to remember my family. Many of the men knew and remembered my father. Some, my mother, even. It was sweet to share memories with them. But then one man mentioned Stephen in one of his stories about Ba and I felt a bell ring in my spirit. I remembered the promise I made to a dying woman. 'Find him,' she said. 'Find him and take his baby to him.' Maybe it wasn't too late to make good on part of that promise. Besides, Stephen was someone who knew my family—who loved my sister and did not know of her terrible fate. What if he was still alive? He deserved to know the truth. I knew with every ounce of my being I must find him.

As it happened, the lieutenant who shared the story was a meticulous fact keeper. He kept a journal during his time in service. In the journal he recorded names of the men who served alongside him, as well as stories and personal information. He was able to find Stephen listed in his journal and email me the information. The last name Stephen gave was Grier. He was from Dayton, Ohio. He used to love to talk about the Wright brothers being from his hometown, the lieutenant recalled. But I have not been able to find one Stephen Grier from Dayton, Ohio—or the surrounding area—who was enlisted during the Vietnam War. Nor was there record of a family by that name residing there. After the Internet came along, I posted on several forums, asking him to contact me. I put the word out anywhere and everywhere I thought he may look. Nothing."

"I don't understand."

"Neither do I. I tried everything. Different spellings, school records, everything I could get my hands on. Everything led to a dead end. Except one possibility that kept coming up."

"Only one?"

"The only one that seemed to make sense. In my research, I found stories of other men. Special forces sent in under cover after the war to find American prisoners of war."

Kay looked her nephew in the eye.

"I don't know, Sam. Maybe I'm crazy. But it seemed to fit. Sky spoke fluent Vietnamese. And why would a journalist risk his life the way Sky did? The way he disappeared so quickly. The promises he made to Thia that I heard through the door. All these things made me wonder. Still make me wonder."

Sam listened in silence, lost in thought. The story had played out in his mind as his aunt told it, like old worn-out, faded movie frames. He was aware of a feeling of disappointment that the search for his father had been a dead end. But he also felt something else: hope. For the moment, this part of the story would have to wait.

"Please tell me how you and my mother came to be on that refugee boat, Dì Kay."

Kay picked a napkin up from the table, folded and unfolded it on her lap. Suddenly she felt very tired. "Ah, yes. This part. This is the hardest," she said softly.

"Mother," Wren interjected gently. "I think it's time to take a break."

Kay waved her daughter off. "I cannot stop now, my child," she said crossly. Then, catching Wren's worried brow, "There's not much more to the story, sweetheart. I'll be fine." Kay sighed heavily and leaned back into her chair.

"I wish we could take a walk. How I do miss talking over a good walk." She looked around at all the expectant eyes upon her. "But this will have to do."

She closed her eyes and saw her sister's face. Her almond eyes, the lift of her smile.

"Thia was small and we were all undernourished, so it was not difficult for her to hide her pregnancy. It wasn't until the middle of February—her seventh month—that I noticed Ma staring at my sister's midsection too often and too long. I was young, but I understood. I knew what was going on. This new shame was more than Ma could bear. She stopped eating again. Thia tried everything to persuade her, but it was no use. All the strength she had gained when Sky was with us seemed to disappear overnight. Thia pleaded with her, wept over her, cajoled...but Ma would just turn away. She stopped speaking. The more Thia's belly swelled, the smaller Ma became.

Thia was remorseful that Ma took her pregnancy so hard. But try as she might, she could not regret being pregnant. She was carrying the child of the man she loved. This filled her whole heart. She came alive like never before. She was even more beautiful." Kay looked softly at Sam. "And she loved you so. She talked to you all the time, told you stories, whispered words of love to you all day long. She was so happy, even when she was sad. She believed Sky would come for her still. For you, though he did not know about you. He had promised her he wouldn't stop until he found a way. She believed. And so she was happy. She glowed from the inside out. She went about her chores humming to herself as she cradled her belly in one arm. Your mother would sing you a lullaby every night."

Kay closed her eyes and in a soft but clear voice sang:

"Dí dầu cầu dáng đống đinh

Cầu tre lắc lẻo ngập ngình khó đi

Khó đi mẹ dắt con đi

Con đi trường học, mẹ đi trường đời"

Sam felt goose bumps lift the hair on his arms. He knew he could not possibly have a memory of this song, but something inside of him sang out in response to its sad, melodic tune.

"What does it mean, Dì Kay?"

Kay lifted tear-filled eyes to meet Sam's. "It is the story of a mother and child crossing a bridge and what awaits them on the other side. The mother takes the child's hand and they meet their fate together."

"And Thia—my mother—would sing this to me?"

"Yes, Sam dear. It was a children's song our own mother sang to us when we were small. But the words took on new meaning to Thia—I think—as her fate became woven together with yours. Uncle Binh was not kind to us, as we cared for Ma in those last days. He blamed Thia for his sister's illness. He was angry at her for bringing disgrace on our family. He let us know in no uncertain terms that when Ma passed, we would no longer be welcome in his home. Uncle began to make plans to send us away." Kay paused and took a deep breath.

"Three and a half years after Ba was taken, our mother died of a broken heart."

Sam let this sink in. He did some quick calculating in his mind.

"Wait, three and a half? So your Ma died in 1979? The year I was born?"

"Ma died on March 20, 1979. A little over a month before we took to the boat—before you were born."

"So she did not know you and Thia were going to try to leave Vietnam?"

Kay shook her head. "Nor did we. Unbeknownst to us, Uncle arranged for our passage on the boat. We did not know his plans until the morning the boat departed. He ordered us to pack a few belongings. We were given some meager food supplies and a flask of water and told to go with him. When we arrived at the docks, Thia realized before I did what was happening. She begged him to let us stay, falling on her knees and weeping at his feet. She knew she was near her due date. That if she left now, Sky would never find her. But the more she begged the more enraged Uncle became. I will never forget how he kicked at her kneeling body. She had wrapped her arms around his legs as she pleaded for our return to the farm. He kicked loose of her hold and spat on the top of her head. He made it clear he did not care if her baby survived. Or if we did either, for that matter. He made a big deal out of the money he had paid for our passage. Said he was giving us our freedom."

Sam could see it all in his mind's eye and he was horrified. He brought his hand up to cover his mouth, speechless. He chest ached from the hard pounding of his heart. It was broken for his mother and his aunt. He glanced at his sister beside him. Sher's face was pale and tear-streaked. She was struggling to swallow a lump in her throat. He put his arm around her and pulled her to him. She buried her face in his shoulder. Kay stirred from her reverie.

"I am sorry. This is a hard story." She looked down and let her own tears fall freely.

Everyone was quiet. Kay showed no sign of continuing her story and Sam realized there was no need. The rest was public record. The drifting boat. The heat of the sun. The pirates who raped and pillaged, leaving the refugees to die. His birth, in blood and tears and sorrow.

Suddenly, he needed to get away from the terrible truth of his beginnings. Sam stood up abruptly and walked out the back door. The others could see him through the plate glass window, staring off into the surrounding hills.

Sher started to push up from the table but Kay gestured softly to the younger woman. "Give him time. He only just discovered his mother. Now he is losing her all over again."

Sher sat back down in her seat and studied Sam's still form through the window. Her brother took out his phone and began tapping a message. "Oh. He will want to talk to Mildred anyway."

Kay glanced at Sam. "Who is Mildred?"

Sher and Scotty looked at each other.

"Mildred is..." Sher began slowly. "Mildred is the woman who inspired The Refugee Tour. She's working with Sam to raise money and awareness for needs of refugees."

Kay studied Sher's face. She could see there was more. Then she turned back to Sam and watched as he talked into the screen of his phone earnestly.

"But who is Mildred to Sam?" Kay said, to the window pane.

Sher also studied her brother through the glass.

"Mildred is the woman he is falling in love with," she said quietly.

"Mildred." Kay repeated the name, as if trying it out on her tongue.

"Dì Kay?"

"Yes, Sher, dear?"

"I'm so sorry. I'm sorry for everything you've been through. I'm sorry about...about Thia. I'm sorry." Sher's voice broke and she lowered her head. Scotty, awkward and still beside her, patted Sher's shoulder clumsily.

"Oh." Kay tipped her head to the side and peered at Sher. "I see my nephew has a kind and compassionate sister. Thank you."

She wiped the corners of her eyes with the napkin again. "This makes me happy. And, Sher?" Kay softly opened her hand toward Sher.

"Yes, Dì Kay?"

"I have always longed for a niece."

~

did you look back, mother?
when the boat was pushed from the shore
and the tide began to carry you?
or were your eyes fixed forward, like Ba's?—
to the other side of the sea—
the other side of the world.

the sunlight knows your face
the earth remembers the imprint of your sole
the hopea trees wait to hear the song
of your voice again
the waves are lapping the sand, they whisper
over and over...your name.

take my hand.
let us cross the bridge together.

LELIA

[july]

(As told and interpreted by the translator Vananiah Vishna)

[The young girl sits in a hard-backed chair with an oversized wooden box on her lap. The box has markings I cannot read and appears very old. She looks younger than the age of twelve I know her to be—thin, frail. Yet, when she begins to speak, her voice holds the weight of many years. She speaks with the wisdom that comes from seeing terrible things.]

"When the desert winds begin to dance and whirl—when you can taste the sand on your tongue and feel the sting of it on your face and the ground beneath you begins to shift—this is when the resurrection flowers take wing. Like the bones of dried up birds remembering to fly, they lift their cracked feet up out of the sand and churn wildly across the sloping dunes. Papa loved collecting the dried resurrection flowers that tumbled through the desert near our home. Do you know the resurrection flower? Papa knew all the names of the flowers and plants. He said they were his friends. But the resurrection flower has other names. My friend Anji calls it the Rose of Jericho. It is not beautiful, like the Damask Rose, but it has a beauty of sorts. Papa loved them. He would inspect each foundling carefully and only bring home those with roots still attached, and thirsty. "Look, Lelia," he would say. "Come watch the plant return to life with me!" Then he would place the dried ball into a bowl of water. It took hours, but the next day, that dried ball of grass had unfolded—opening like a kestrel unfurling her wings—waking up from a deep sleep. The limbs greening out like feathers and opening to reveal the tiny seeds the plant was protecting in her belly. Papa would pick the seeds, one by one. Some, he would plant, but the others would go into his seed collection. Into this box. See?"

[The child opens the hinged lid of the box and offers for me to look inside. I inspect the seeds. So many! All different colors and sizes—each carefully labeled in neat script. After a moment I gently steer her back to my original question: "Lelia, I know it is hard. But can you tell me more? About what happened the day you went to meet your brother?" She fingers the seeds a little while longer, palms a few of the larger ones that look like sunflower seeds to me. Suddenly, this young face takes on the shadow of an old woman's face.]

"My father brought only this collection of seeds when we were forced to run away. Over the years he had collected and carefully dried his favorite blossoms until he had many sleeping plants. He kept his collection in here, in grandpa's old toolbox. Father said these are the tools of his trade."

[The child swallows hard and closes the lid of the box.]

"They took my brother a year before we had to flee. Loran played the *tembûr*—he made such lovely music. Some days my grandpa would go with him to nearby villages to make money playing his songs. That is what they were doing when the men came through that village. They killed my grandfather and took Loran. They wanted him to make music only for them. He was fifteen years old. Six months after they took him Loran was able to contact our father. He was no longer only their musician but was training to be a soldier.

I know these things only because I listened in secret as mama and papa talked in the night. They could not find a way to bring my brother home safely. Mama often cried when she thought we weren't paying attention. Vian and I missed our big brother. But soon we stopped speaking Loran's name. It carried too much sorrow.

Our home was in the village of Khana Sor. I lived there all my life. We had a nice home. Mama made it nice. It always smelled of naan and spices and so many good things. When word came the soldier men were coming, we fled on foot into the mountains. We left everything, except for food and a few clothes. Mama said when it was safe we would come back for our other things. I left my good shoes. Vian cried after her special dolly. We hid in the mountains with others from our village for many days. We ran out of food and water. We ate the leaves of trees. Finally, papa decided with some of the other men that we must leave or die. Many had already died of thirst or hunger. We walked for three days until we crossed the border. After another two weeks we walked more until we crossed another border. Papa told me we were in a new country—a place called Turkey. There we were put into a camp by the policemen who met us and gave us blankets, food and water. I was only ten then, older than Vian even now. She was six, so small our mother carried her everywhere. Papa carried this box.

We waited for two years in the camp. Every day my father was trying to find a safer place for us. Finally, we were told we had a sponsor in the United States. We were going to the same city where Uncle Deniz and Aunt Mîna lived. We were going to live with Miss Mildred and Miss Cindy. They made a place for us.

A safe place. A place where papa could grow flowers; a place with a big kitchen for mama to cook her recipes. A place where Vian could play dolls and papa could teach me more about growing things.

But the nearer the time drew for us to leave, the more mama and papa began to despair about leaving my brother. Somehow, I do not know these things, somehow papa got word to Loran that we were leaving the country. Loran arranged a secret meeting so we could all see him one last time. It was very dangerous for him. We could not tell anyone. We had to go back across one border, into a land called Syria. Loran was able to arrange for a car so papa could drive us to meet him. We told our friends and neighbors in the camp that we were going to a nearby camp because we'd gotten word some of our family was there. We left just before dark. The car was waiting for us, hidden outside the busy town. I don't think the drive was too long, but it seemed so because of the silence. Even Vian was quiet—afraid of the fear on mama and papa's faces. We drove into an old factory. It looked like no one was there but there were some lights. Papa drove to the place where Loran was to meet us. When he walked out from behind a small metal building, mama started to cry. She started to open her door to run to my brother, but papa stopped her. "Delal, we must wait!" He said. "It may not be safe. Loran will give us the signal." Mama sat, whimpering. I could see her hands trembling. Just as Loran raised his hand to summon us, we saw movement behind him. "Something is wrong," Papa said. A man came out of the darkness, but my brother did not see him. "Stay!" Papa said, opening his door. "Loran!" He yelled to my brother. "Behind you!"

The man had a gun. I heard him insult my brother. Then he

shot papa in the head. We watched papa's body fall. There was screaming. It was a while before I realized it was my own. Loran had a gun too. He shot the man and ran to us. Climbing in the car where papa had so recently sat, he drove us away so fast. All I could think was my papa was still back there on the ground. But there was no time to get him. As we raced away, more men appeared out of the dark and there was more gunfire. Loran drove us back across the border. We came to the place outside the city where we had picked up the car. He stopped and told mama that he had to leave us there. Mama begged him to come with us but he refused, telling her that he could not keep us safe now. He said many other things to mama, but I did not understand. She kissed him and held onto him and wept. We were behind an old shed and Loran took me and Vian around to the front of the building. He hugged us and kissed us and told us to take care of mama. He said he must go and take care of papa now. He told us to wait for mama, that he had something he needed to tell her before leaving. We waited, as we were told. After a little while, we heard a gunshot. It sounded very close. Very close. Vian started to cry and I put my arms around her. Shortly after that, mama came for us. We walked back to the camp in silence.

Mama has not spoken a word since that night."

MILDRED

[july]

"Yes."

"Mildred, you should *consider*. Give this some time before you answer. There's no race to decide. You and Cindy should talk about what this means."

"Cindy?"

Cindy squeezed Mildred's hand.

"I agree."

Valisha studied the determined faces of the two women sitting across from her. She shook her head and pushed away from the desk. "I don't know." She walked to the window and looked out on the quiet street below. Almost everyone in the city was gone for the day. She'd put off this meeting as long as she could. The sun shimmered its way down the capitol dome.

She knew Mildred Ruffner. Knew the stubbornness of the woman. She just couldn't get a feeling in her gut for what was right. She'd talked to Deniz. He still wanted his sister to come—more than ever. His heart was broken for her and his nieces. But was this the best idea? Did these two women know what it would take to begin again in life when facing this kind of brokenness?

She turned to face Mildred and Cindy. "Look. We're talking about PTSD here. This family left everything. Had to flee for their lives. And in the midst of that bit of ugly, these two girls witnessed their father's murder. Delal may have seen her son shoot himself. Hell, he may have asked her to do it! You two were looking for help with your business—while assisting a family in the meantime. What you are getting is a far cry from what we promised. I've sent word to some colleagues in Germany who are have more experience with this type of trauma. But we don't have any professionals here in West Virginia who have the kind of experience with this technique we need." She leaned on her desk and looked first Mildred and then Cindy in the eye. "This is new territory for us. I don't know what you'd be getting into if you invite this family into your life."

Mildred returned Valisha's stare. "Valisha. We have been *waiting* for this family. We've prepared a home for them. Every detail put into that house was done with Delal and Lelia and Vian and...and Deza in mind. My Aunt Juanita sewed a Teddy bear by hand for Vian. It's red—her favorite color. We've stocked Lelia's shelves with art supplies and field guides. We've studied their profiles and know them by heart. We've dreamed for this family." A single tear slid down Mildred's cheek. "They need us now more than ever. You say this is not a race, but what if we'd been able to bring them here sooner? These two girls might still have a father. Delal might still have her husband. What other kind of dangers will they face while we consider how their presence in our lives will jeopardize our comfort? The only family they have left is here in Charleston. The longer we wait, the greater the chance for more tragedy. How can we change our minds now?"

Valisha dropped her eyes. She studied the contents of her desktop blindly. Stapler. Tape dispenser. A picture of Julianne. The small purple porcelain pig her co-workers gave her last year for her birthday. She loved pigs. An open file gaped up at her. The Agha family smiled into thin air, hope swelling in their eyes.

SAM & MILDRED

[july-august]

He'd never seen someone look so beautiful in tears. The need to hold her was a sharp pain through the core of his being. Mildred's eyes glistened, pools of moonlight.

"Sam, I feel so helpless. How could this happen?"

She folded onto her side and let her cheek sink into the pillow, let out a quivery sigh. "I so wish you were here."

He touched her face on the screen. A pain moved through his chest and into his throat. "Me too, Mil. Me too." She closed her eyes. "You need to get some rest, Moonflower. You've had a long day. We can talk more in the morning. But think about this: tomorrow we fly out to Connecticut, then is Rhode Island. Then I have four days off. What would you think about me making a quick trip down there, like we tried to plan before?"

Mildred spoke with her eyes closed. "Yes, please."

He waited for her to say more but she was silent. He chuckled. "Try not to be so excited."

A slow smile arched gently up and she opened her eyes. "I'm afraid to get excited. You don't know how disappointed I was last time. Do you really think you could?"

"Let me put Scott on it and I'll get you the details. I can't think of a better way to spend those days off."

"Dreamy wonderful." Mildred closed her eyes again. "Yes, let me know the details. We're always ready for guests. Sam, I'm so tired. How was Kay today?"

"She seemed good. Wren says meeting me has given her new strength, though her health is still failing fast. I've spoken with her every day since, but I feel this strange sort of emptiness being away from her. It's like…it's like I've found a piece of myself that I never knew was missing."

Mildred yawned and burrowed deeper into the pillow. "Well, really, that's exactly what happened." She tried to open her eyes but they kept drifting closed.

"I wish there was a way I could bring Dì Kay on tour with me. I wish I could play some music for her."

"Mmm. Why don't you play a song for her on FaceTime? Like you do for me. That would be nice."

He tried to memorize the way her dark lashes looked against her cheeks when her eyes were closed. "You need some rest so I'll let you go." He hesitated. "Mildred?"

"Mmm."

"I really wish I could have been with you. Today. When you found out about Deza. I'm so sorry. I wish I could be there now."

Mildred did not fight the thought of his arms holding her. "Will you sing me my song before you go?"

"Always." He picked up the guitar and started strumming.

la de da— la de da— la de dada de

forget about the sky, she said, pointing to the moon.
she closed the curtains way up tight, said
sleep is coming soon.

so close your little eyes,

my love, and
dream your little dreams

the world is filled with lullabies
some are heard, some are seen...

and as you sleep,
the earth keeps turning
the ocean depths continue churning
trails of stars continue burning, above you...

so dream your little dreams,
my love,
and as you sleep

your heart keeps beating
the birds above continue singing
the night and day continue meeting
and I——I will never leave you.

so close your little eyes, my love, and
dream your little dreams, my love
I give you quiet lullabies
and I will never leave...

la de da—— la de da——   la de dada de

Sam let his voice trail off but continued to play softly as he watched Mildred smile with her eyes closed. Then he was there beside her, sinking into the coverlet, holding her with his song.

~

"Bear's or the Grille?"

They were standing on the corner of Front Street and Columbus, right down from Infinity Hall. He'd been rehearsing all morning with Brit, Dan and Rob—preparing for the show. This was his first time playing this venue and he wasn't quite happy with the sound. He'd been puzzling over the amp configuration when suddenly, there she was. It always took a while to get his head out of the music and back into the real world, but this? She'd surprised him—arranged it with the guys. "Just go, man," Dan had said. "I'll figure out the sound."

He touched her hand to make sure she was real.

She smiled, her cheeks plumper than he remembered, and squeezed his hand. "Earth to Gillenwater. What are you hungry for? Barbecue at Bear's or something more upscale in the cozier Grille?"

Sam shifted his weight, then cupped her chin in one hand, studied the sky in her eyes. The late morning sun played cloud shadows over her skin. She glowed under his gaze, staring right back. The rings under her eyes were gone and he could tell she had gained weight. Her hair was shorter—the usually unruly kinky curls tamed into submission, styled up into a sleek, soft afro. They stood just so until her eyes filled and she threw her arms around him.

"Damn, Gillenwater, it's good to see you. I've missed you."

He returned her embrace, buried his face in her springy hair and breathed in its clean scent. "I've missed you too, Heather. I've missed you too."

They grabbed some barbeque to go and crossed a block to

the Wadsworth Atheneum Museum. Heather led him to a table on the grounds shaded by a copse of Honey Locust trees. A giant reddish-orange abstract sculpture chaperoned their picnic. Sam paused to take it in before sitting.

"We call him 'Stego,'" Heather grinned. "He's been here since 1973." She gazed up at the abstract stegosaurus. "I love him. This is one of my favorite places to come and think."

Sam opened his box and took a messy bite of his sandwich, lifting his eyes again to the spiny-looking creature. "He's pretty impressive," he said, with his mouth full. He hadn't realized how hungry he was. "I'm glad to see you've found a friend."

Heather laughed and it sounded so real Sam stopped mid-bite and looked at her long. Catching his gaze, Heather paused.

"What?" she asked self-consciously.

Sam smiled. "Nothing. You just sound good. You look good, Heather."

Heather studied her food. "I *am* good." She set the sandwich down in the box and took a sip of iced tea. "I know it hasn't been that long, but it feels like I'm finding myself again, Gil." She tilted her head and looked at him. "I've been happy."

"I'm glad, Heather."

They finished eating in quiet, letting the sound of the fountain under Stego fill the space of a million questions between them. Then she cleared the table and went over to Sam's side, leaned her head on his shoulder. He draped one arm around her.

"I've been following your refugee tour on Facebook. You're doing something wonderful, Gil. I'm so proud of you. And I read the story about your aunt. I can't imagine what it must mean to have found her. I'm sorry she's sick. A lot has happened in your life since we were together."

The shadows of the moving leaves rustling above them looked like water rippling along the concrete courtyard. Mildred's face shimmered through the lightplay.

"Yeah, a lot has happened."

"Dan tells me you've met someone."

Sam hesitated. Heather twined her fingers through his on her lap. "It's okay." She whispered, turning her mouth to his ear. "I'm going to be okay."

He looked down at her. "I know you are, Heather."

She turned her face away from Sam's. "Look, Sam, there's something I need to give you."

She pulled a folded envelope from her back pocket and tucked it in his hands.

"What's this?" he asked, puzzled.

"It's yours," she said, avoiding his eyes. Sam opened the envelope and unfolded the paper inside. He looked at Heather over the words of the poem she'd taken from his journal. She smiled tremulously and he felt the full impact of her beside him. He folded the paper again, tucked it inside the envelope and slipped it back into her warm hands.

"These words are for you, Heather."

MILDRED

[july-august]

Lelia came first, the ghost of a smile leading her, serenely pulling a lavender-colored carry-on. Delal and Vian followed, the smaller girl clinging to her mother's hand, Delal struggling under a heavy backpack.

At the sight of them, a cheer broke out amongst the little crowd waiting. When Delal saw her brother, she burst into tears. Deniz rushed over and engulfed her in his arms.

"*Ez li vir im. Ez li vir im.* I am here. I am here, dear sister," he whispered over and over into her hair as silent sobs wracked her body.

Mildred and Cindy hovered in the background as the Yezidi community that accompanied them flocked around the small family. Cindy, arms filled with a large bouquet of flowers, glanced nervously at Mildred. Mildred smiled at her over the head of the hand-made teddy bear in her arms. "It's okay," she mouthed.

Suddenly, Lelia's heart-shaped face peeked at them from a gap in the huddle. She wrested herself free of the others' arms and legs and bodies and demurely walked over to Mildred and Cindy. She stood directly in front of them, then pulled her arms behind her back and, smiling shyly, said, "Ms. Mil-dred, Ms. Cin-day, I love you."

Mildred wrapped the girl in her arms, teddy bear and all. Through tears she said, "Oh, Lelia! We love you too!" She leaned back, held the girl at arm's length and whispered, "Beautiful." Cindy wrapped one arm around Lelia, who leaned into the hug. Then they were joined by Vian, who stood behind her sister and peeked at the two women.

Mildred held out the teddy bear to her. "For you, Vian."

Vian's eyes were shining as she reached out and hugged the bear to her. "*Sipas ji were,*" she said sweetly.

When Mildred looked up, she saw all the adults were watching them. She locked eyes with Delal, who had fresh tears streaming down her face. The girls' mother stepped forward, placed her hands together in a gesture of honor, and bowed slightly to Mildred and Cindy. Deniz stepped beside her.

"My sister wishes to thank you. She thanks you for her life, and for the lives of her daughters."

Delal straightened up and approached Mildred. She took Mildred's face in her hands and looked searchingly into her eyes. Then she kissed both of Mildred's cheeks. Turning to Cindy, she did the same. Cindy thrust the bouquet into Delal's hands.

"*Slav, bi xêr hatî!* Hello, welcome!" She gave their guest the one phrase she and Mildred had been practicing in Kurmanji. Hearing their native tongue tumble clumsily from this American woman's mouth made everyone smile, and a chorus of cheers rang out.

Mildred smiled.

"Come," she said. "Let's get you to your new home."

~

The girls were wound up. Though they had been traveling for several days and should have been exhausted, they ran from room to room to room in the little house, talking excitedly to each other as they went. Mildred and Cindy walked Delal and Deniz through, letting Deniz translate as they explained where things were and how the household was set up.

The refrigerator and cupboards were stocked with typical Yezidi foods. Mîna and some of the other women had been cooking all day and had prepared a most delicious welcome. There were platters of dolma—the stuffed grape leaves Lelia adored, boiled kibbeh, and a crock of mierr waiting. And if those dishes did not warm their hearts and tummies and make them feel at home, Mîna had also labored over a platter of baklava and what looked like date and nut cookies she called *kulicha*.

Mildred nibbled a piece of baklava as the little group moved down the hall toward the bedrooms. The sweetness of the phyllo melted on her tongue and she thought she'd never tasted anything so close to heaven. She nudged Cindy and gestured to the sweet treat in her hand.

"We need Mîna's recipe!" she mouthed. Cindy nodded. "I thought the same thing," she mouthed back.

"And this," Mildred said, sliding the pocket doors at the end of the hallway, "is Lelia and Vian's room."

Deniz called the girls and spoke firmly to them as they came giggling into the hall. When Deniz explained this was where they would sleep, they both grew quiet. Mildred gestured for them to look around. For all the giggling they had done earlier, they were strangely silent as they took in their room. Vian, who was still carrying the teddy bear, walked over to the twin bed with a red patchwork quilt on it—the same patchwork design as her bear. She sat down on the edge and looked up, then gestured towards her chest and said, "*Bo min?*"

Mildred looked questioningly at Deniz, who smiled down at his niece. "She wants to know if this is for her."

Mildred smiled and nodded. "Yes. Yes, for you." She gestured to the bed and to the little girl. "All for you."

Deniz translated what Mildred said. "*Sipas ji were,*" the girl whispered. Then she lay on her side and hugged the bear tight to her chest. She closed her eyes and breathed, "*Ez jê hez dikim! Ew bedew e.*"

Deniz said, "She thanks you. She loves it very much and says it is beautiful."

Delal went and sat on the edge of the bed. She smoothed Vian's face with her long fingers and kissed her forehead. Vian did not open her eyes but said, "*Ez ji te hez dikim, mama.*"

Deniz grinned at Mildred and Cindy. "It seems the day has finally caught up with my young niece."

As Vian dozed, all eyes sought Lelia. Cindy had chosen a botanical theme for her side of the room, knowing how the girl loved helping her father in his work of growing things. Mildred had placed a bouquet of dried lavender on her pillow, tied with a gauzy ribbon. The girl sat on her bed holding this bouquet, tears streaming down her face.

"*Ez dadgeh dikim,*" Lelia said, between soft sniffs.

Delal rushed over to her older daughter and hugged her to her breast. They cried together.

Deniz watched his sister comfort her daughter. "Lelia misses her father," he said weakly.

Through all this, Delal did not speak one word.

~

Petey was happiest of all to have the girls in residence. He had not been permitted to greet the family the night of their arrival, as Mildred did not know how Yezidi culture considered dogs. She needn't have worried. Every morning at six a.m., Delal walked with her girls to the big house. And Petey waited by the kitchen door to greet them. Vian and Lelia lavished him with hugs and kisses, belly rubs and snacks. Pete trailed their every step, wagging his tail behind.

While Delal and Cindy worked with the kitchen staff and around the house, Lelia and Vian joined Mildred and the grounds crew in their morning rounds. They helped water the gardens, pick fresh flowers for the house, weed and fertilize, even milk the cows. The girls were no strangers to hard work. This Mildred learned very quickly. And they were eager to help, eager to learn. With every new task their vocabulary expanded.

"Cow," Mildred said, as they scooped grain into Meredith's trough.

"Cow?" The girls repeated dutifully, followed by a fit of giggles as Meredith nuzzled their fingers with soft lips.

"Water," Mildred said, as she filled buckets with the garden hose.

"Wa-ter?" They repeated, dipping their hands in.

Sometimes the girls would gesture to objects, asking for a name.

"Tree."

"Butterfly."

"Sky."

"Cloud."

Lelia was not satisfied with "flower." She wanted to know the specific names of all of the blooms in the gardens. Her memory amazed Mildred. She was touched by the tender way the older girl handled the flowers.

Daisy, coxcomb, basil, goldenrod, bachelor's button, violet, sunflower, lavender, verbena, lisianthus, poppy...nothing escaped notice.

A gamechanger came when Mildred and Cindy decided—with Delal's permission—the girls needed a cellphone to share. Just in case. For safety. One day, Lelia came home from the culture center ebullient. One of her teachers helped her find a flower identification app. She took the phone with her everywhere, and was often found capturing images for identification. Vian just rolled her eyes. She was much more interested in the barn cat and her kittens.

Both girls approached each day with an eagerness and gladness that filled Mildred with wonder. Their gratitude was as thick and soft as their long, dark hair, which Mildred was currently trying to tame.

Vian sat on the floor—Pete curled up between her legs—in front of Mildred as she raked the hairbrush through the girl's unruly hair, trying not to pull.

"Oww!" Pete gave Vian's arm a concerned sniff.

"Well, you certainly have that down," Mildred muttered, backing off her efforts. "Honestly. What do you do in your sleep every night? How do you get so many tangles?" She leaned forward and made a gesture of scissors with her fingers.

"No, Mil-dred!" Vian laughed at her teasing. She handed Mildred an elastic to tie back her locks.

"I do give up." Mildred took the ponytail holder and scooped Vian's hair back into one long bundle, deftly securing it with the elastic. She took the brush and smoothed out the ponytail, reluctant for this time together to end. Already these girls had filled a place in her heart. She remembered Valisha's words. *Your life will never be the same again.* It was true. Her life would never be the same. There had already been many challenges, but also, such sweetness. She twined a loose curl around her finger and gave it a gentle tug. "There! Now, at least you're presentable."

Vian gently nudged Pete off her lap and turned to face Mildred. Mildred looked into the girl's face, smitten. She was always taken aback by the soft curve of cheeks, the glow of smooth brown skin, eyes—two dark lights. She so wanted to photograph this face. Vian kissed Mildred on the cheek. "I love you!" Then she wiggled out of Mil's grasp and inspected herself in the mirror.

Lelia giggled beside her sister, tying her own hair back and surveying her handiwork from all sides in the mirror.

"Hurry, we'll be late!" Mildred pulled Vian's ponytail and scuttled out of the room. Every day after chores, she drove them into town to the culture center. Here they were being schooled in the English language and other elements of American culture, as well as their own customs and ways. And here, Delal was learning sign language. To make it possible to converse with Delal, Mildred, Cindy and the rest of the staff were also studying sign language. Two afternoons a week Mrs. Perris from the culture center came out to the farm and instructed them. Lelia and Vian were learning sign, too. It was brilliant, really; bridging the language gap for them all.

Doctors had examined Delal's vocal chords and could find no physical reason she couldn't speak. When asked in her native tongue to try to explain what the problem was, Delal would simply point to her throat, open her mouth, and shake her head. She could not make her voice come out.

~

When Mildred returned from the culture center, the kitchen was cool and gleaming from a recent scrubbing. The table looked honeyed in the sunlight. Cinnamon scent lingered. She walked through the empty dining room into the sunroom and found Petey in his favorite sunspot. He wagged his tail but didn't bother to get up. She watched the sun lift up over the south lawn. The heat left a haze on the horizon, the sky a chalky blue. Cindy would be up at the Glasshouse, beginning preparations for the wedding reception they were hosting tomorrow. She would head up there to help soon, but she needed a quiet moment first.

She missed him.

They didn't have their regular FaceTime last night because the show ran too late. She was just too exhausted to wait. It was a quick text into dead air, telling him she was heading for bed. And now she missed him. This insistent ache inside of her frightened her a little.

How did this happen? Wasn't she the woman who didn't need a man?

Mildred shook her head. How had she let herself fall for him? There was too much unsaid between them. Some days the entire thing felt crazy. Impossible. Yet, she didn't want... What didn't she want? She didn't want to startle this away by needing him. But she thought about him every second. She carried him with her wherever she went.

Mildred sighed and pulled the iPad off its charger. Maybe she could find some highlights from the Connecticut show. Maybe seeing him, hearing him, would calm this storm inside. She pulled up the entertainment news app that had become a constant in her repertoire and searched his name. Mildred tapped on the first result and settled back into the cushions of the overstuffed chair.

The segment opened up with footage of Sam singing an acoustic version of "Oddbird." Mildred smiled at his lonely image in the spotlight. Suddenly, the stage lights went crazy and Sam was joined onstage by several unfamiliar faces, each playing an instrument. "Ladies and gentlemen," Sam announced, "please welcome Epic Quest!" The audience screamed as the band turned Oddbird's sweet melody into an epic adventure ballad. A woman's voice spoke over the video.

"The audience of Sam Gillenwater's concert in Hartford, Connecticut last night was treated to a surprise appearance by Connecticut natives Epic Quest. The pop culture band is rumored to be a favorite of Gillenwater's manager, Scott Chambers, who is a regular Comic Con attendee. Epic Quest added their own personal style to the title song from Gil's latest album, *Oddbird*, and Gil sang their song "Adventure Road" with them in encore. The band's lead singer, Len Sonnel, paid tribute to Gil's Refugee Tour, thanking the rumored Grammy nominee for taking the lead in tackling a dire social issue."

The video cut to a close-up of, presumably, Len Sonnel, caught mid-sentence. "... and America is made up of immigrants. Imagine what this country would be like if people like Gil were not a part of it. Less music, less art, less imagination. Less love. If you appreciate the rich variation in culture, excellence, and beauty in America...why not support this cause? Pull up Gil's Facebook page right now. Click on the GoFundMe link and lend your support..." Gil joined the singer in the spotlight, extended his hand and then pulled him into a hug. The video cut to the reporter, sitting at her desk. "Epic Quest band members were not the only natives to welcome Gil to Connecticut." A still picture flashed on the screen. An image of a couple sitting at a picnic table. The woman's head was on the man's shoulder. His arm draped across her. Mildred felt the blood drain from her face. "We caught this shot of Sam Gillenwater canoodling with ex-girlfriend, Heather Watts. Our investigators discovered that Watts has been staying with her parents in her hometown of Hartford since her heroin overdose several weeks ago. Is their relationship on the mend? Only time will tell."

Mildred closed the iPad.

~

"Do you believe," Cindy asked Mildred, "that Delal's muteness really is psychological?"

"What else could it be, C?"

They were outside the Glasshouse, putting finishing touches on the banquet tables for the wedding reception. Delal was at the big house, supervising staff and getting a start on the dinner they would serve. Cindy folded napkins as they spoke, arranged the place settings just so.

"I don't know. I know that sometimes after a stroke people lose their speech. Maybe all the trauma she witnessed could cause a stroke of sorts? It just seems so...hard to accept, that this is an emotional thing."

Mildred studied her friend's face. Worry lined her forehead.

"Valisha says it's not unheard of. Trauma can affect people in so many different ways. It makes sense. I mean, if Delal could talk, she would have to tell her story. Losing her son. Forced to leave her home. Hiding in the mountains. Almost starving to death. Watching her children suffer. Witnessing the murder of her husband and the suicide of her son? Who wants to tell that story?"

"I know you're right," Cindy said. "I just wish I knew how to help her. I thought she would feel safe here and maybe open up to us. Sometimes, when I watch her working, I feel her grief like a knife—you know? So, so sharp. But then the girls come in and it's a visible balm. I can see the change in her. And I think she will speak. Any second, she will find her voice. But she doesn't. And I wonder, will she do this for them? You know they must miss their mother's voice. Lelia says she used to sing to them every night. That she has a beautiful voice."

Mildred placed a Mason jar filled with wild flowers on the table. "Do you think I should just do one in the center? Or a row down the middle?" She stepped back and surveyed her handiwork. "Definitely more down the middle." She returned to their catering trailer and pulled out some pint jars and buckets of cut flowers. As she made the floral arrangements she struggled to find words for Cindy.

"I think we *are* helping her, C. She is safe here and so are her children. I believe she does trust us. But the way I understand PTSD is that it changes your brain. Valisha is still trying to find a psychologist with the experience to help. She's waiting to hear about a grant she applied for to see if they can afford to bring someone in for a time. She really wants an expert to come and stay a while and train some others in that narrative exposure therapy."

"I don't even know what that is. Why does she think that will work?"

"It's a therapy technique that somehow uses storytelling. From what I've read, the therapist helps a person create a storyline of her life—the good, the bad and the ugly all laid out together. They use concrete things, like flowers and stones, to symbolize the good and bad events throughout their life. It gives them a picture of the fuller story of their life. Or something like that. Valisha says they've had some success treating refugees with it in Germany. That's why she wants to try it here."

"I hope she gets the grant."

"Me too."

They were quiet. Mildred heard a chickadee singing her sweet song. It made her think of Sam. She wrinkled her brow and focused harder on the flowers. Cindy moved around the table, using raffia to tie a few sprigs of lavender to each place setting of silverware. She glanced up at Mildred.

"You okay? You're awful quiet today."

"Maybe."

"What's going on, Mil? Is it Sam? I noticed you haven't Face-Timed these past two nights. Did the two of you have a fight or something?"

Mildred pinched a leaf off a sunflower and dropped her hands to her sides.

"I'm just trying to figure some things out."

Cindy watched Mildred rearrange the flowers five different ways.

"You know I'm always here if you want to talk."

Mildred sighed and sat down in one of the slipcovered chairs.

"I know. I just...I just don't really know what to say. I've been having second thoughts about things. Feeling like this thing with Sam—whatever it is—can never work. And, do I want to risk trying? I mean, what if this means nothing to him? What if it's all just a game?"

Cindy put down a bundle of lavender and walked over. She sat beside Mildred and took her hand.

"Listen to me. It's okay to be afraid. Love does that. I know you've been hurt before, Mil. You've kept your heart locked up for so long now. But I've seen how happy you've been these past weeks. I've seen how faithful Sam has been. I mean, how many guys take the time to video call every night? Every night, Mil. I've heard him sing to you and make you laugh, I've heard how you share about things that really matter to you. Just ask yourself, and really think about all you've shared with this man so far—just ask yourself if this is the kind of guy who takes other people's feelings for granted. I don't think so. I really don't, Mil. Look what he's done—meeting his aunt and cousin. This is a guy who cares about people. And Sam cares about you. You can't hold him accountable for what happened with Levi. You can't let the past keep you from having a future."

A single tear slid down Mildred's cheek and she studied her hand in Cindy's.

"It's been fifteen years."

"I know, sweetheart."

"I thought I was over all that."

"What woman gets over being left at the altar? No matter how much time goes by. Besides, you haven't let any man close enough to test it out, whether your heart is healed yet or not."

"I swore I never would again."

"I remember."

Mildred breathed in a shaky breath.

"Cindy, Levi and I grew up together. I loved him my entire life. How could I not know him? How could I not have seen what was coming? And if I could miss something so monumental in

Levi, how can I really know Sam? Is it possible to know someone you've only met in person one time?"

"Mental illness doesn't make sense, Mil. Neither does addic-
tion. You know this. And September 11 affected us all so deeply.
It just triggered something in Levi he couldn't come back from.
What happened to Levi has nothing to do with Sam, Mildred."

Mildred was quiet, lost in memory. "I tried so hard to find
him. To get him the treatment he needed."

"I know."

"Even the PI dad hired told me to give up. That it was too
dangerous. The militia too unstable."

"I know."

Mildred covered her face with her hands and groaned quietly.
"I hate this! I thought I was through with all this."

Cindy patted Mil's hand. "Is this really about what happened
with Levi? You haven't dated at all since he left. Then you get
involved in a relationship with someone online. Maybe it felt
safer? Less real? And now, it's almost time for Sam to come here.
Almost time for this relationship to go to another level. What
are you afraid of, Mil?"

Cindy's words seeped like a frigid draft under the door of
Mildred's heart. She felt brittle, a piece of thin ice.

"I just can't help wondering what I have to offer someone
like Sam. I mean, I've made a conscious choice to stay rooted
here. Wouldn't it make more sense for him to be with someone
who could travel with him, support his career with her physical
presence? I'm just thinking that if I put an end to this thing now,
it might save us both a lot of heartache later." Mildred looked at
Cindy. "The trouble is, I think it's too late for me. I can't bear the
thought of waking up each morning and not hearing his voice.

I can't bear to think of going to sleep without his face being the last thing I see."

Tears were flowing freely now. Cindy wrapped Mildred in her arms and kissed the top of her head.

"I think you're overthinking, Mil. People in show business do this all the time. Love knows no distance. You're just scared. And that's okay. But you need to talk to Sam about this. It's not fair to shut him out like you've been doing. And it's not like you." Cindy held her friend at arm's length and looked her in the eye. "You need to talk to him. Promise me?"

Mildred nodded, still weepy. "I promise."

SAM & MILDRED

[august-september]

"Mil, I would have told you about seeing Heather. If you'd given me a chance to explain. She surprised me. I had no idea..."

"I know, Sam."

There was a detached quality in her voice that filled him with wildness. Already she sounded far away.

"Nothing happened. Just two old friends catching up. That picture you saw, it was misleading, it made it look more than what it was..."

"I believe you."

"She just put her head on my shoulder for a second. I swear, they must have been hiding in the bushes just waiting..."

"I'm sure they were."

"So, you believe me?"

"Of course."

"Then...I'm confused. I don't understand. So, nothing has changed, right?"

"Something has changed for me."

"What? What, Mildred? Because I still feel the same as I did three days ago. This was just a misunderstanding. The press does this all the time   confuses reality with fiction."

Mildred drew a shaky breath. *Why? Why was she doing this?* She closed her eyes and remembered the sear through her heart when she saw the picture. It made her want to run away.

"I know this doesn't seem fair. But I just need a little time."

"Will you please let me come down and spend some time with you? Or, better yet, why don't you fly up here and be with me? I have four days off before Portland. Please?"

"Sam, are you listening to me? I said I think we need some time. *I* need some time."

"This is crazy. Let me FaceTime you. I need to see your face when you say this to me."

She knew if she saw his face her resolve would crumble.

That one lock of hair always falling in his eyes. His fingers taming it back into place...

"No." She said it too firmly—could almost feel him flinch. She softened her voice. "We've talked about this, Sam. I—I don't trust myself. When I see you I can't think clearly."

He had to convince her this was madness.

"All I want is to be with you, Mildred. You are the only person I want to be with. So why are we having this conversation? Just catch a flight. We can spend the next two days on the shore. There's a lighthouse. Lobster and the ocean and you. That's all I need."

Mildred wanted to cry. It seemed like that's all she'd been doing lately.

"But see, that's just it, Sam. I don't have the kind of life where I can drop everything to be with you. We have seven weddings in August. Seven. Plus, the rooms are sold out for the next four weeks. Plus, the girls, Sam. And Delal. I have to be here for them. I can't leave Cindy with all this right now. Even if I thought it was the best thing."

Even if? Sam was silent. Too fretful for a mind trick. How could he imagine happy and calm when it felt like the bottom was falling out of his world?

"Sam?"

"I just…I don't know what to say. I know we don't, well, we haven't, talked about the future but I thought we would get there eventually." His voice was husky. "I don't want to think about tomorrow without you in it."

Mildred hesitated.

"Sam—I—I'm not saying it won't, but, in the end, I just don't know if whatever this is will work. You asked me once why I'm not married. The truth is, I almost was. Fifteen years ago I was to marry a boy I knew all my life. He grew up over the mountain from me. He had all my loves. My friendship love, my sister love, my passionate love, my 'I'm going to grow old with you' love… And when tragedy struck, he left. Turned into someone I didn't even recognize. This boy I had known all my life, Sam. I don't think I can live through pain like that again. How can I really know you, Sam? When the time we've been together is so… so *not* the kind of time it takes to know someone? Really know someone. I mean, like what if you talk in your sleep and it drives me crazy? What if it annoys you that I take long showers? What if you hate the way my big toe leans into my second toe?"

"I've seen your toes, Moonflower. And I love them."

"You know what I mean, Sam. All the little things that make up a person. Their mannerisms and smells and habits and, oh, I don't know! Everything that comes from rubbing shoulders together through life. Not a screen. Flesh. And. Blood.

When I saw that picture of you and Heather—this is so hard to say out loud—when I saw that picture, it scared me—how much it hurt. And then I started thinking about my life and yours and how hard it will be to make this work when we can't be together the way...the way you were with Heather on that park bench and I guess I just..."

"Now, hold on just a minute. You just...this is a lot, Mildred."

"I know."

Sam closed his eyes and breathed in deeply.

"Let me take these one at a time."

"Okay."

Mildred swallowed tears and waited.

"First, I'm sorry you've been hurt by someone. I don't know what kind of man could ever walk away from you, Mildred. I want to hear that story. But not like this. I want to look into your eyes as you tell it. I want to be able to hold you, to be there and show you that I'm not going anywhere. I know I can't do that over the phone, but Mildred? This is how it is right now. This is how we've made our beginning. It's not how I want the rest of our story to go. I know my life is crazy right now. I mean, the album. And the tour. The refugee fund. And I just found my birth family. But it's not always like this. And even when I'm on the road, there are ways to be with the people I care about. Don't you think I want that? There has just been too much other stuff lately...I would never—NEVER—ask you to give up the life you've made. The beauty you create everywhere you go is one of the things that makes you so beautiful. And what you're doing with Delal and the girls? It's...amazing. *You* are amazing. I can't say it enough."

Mildred waited, heart pounding.

"And, how do you really know anyone, Mil? I can't promise I'll never change. Hell, I don't want to promise that. I hope we both keep changing and growing. Together. All I can say is this.

When I'm with you? I feel like I'm more *me* than I've ever been in my life. I want to be a better person because of you. Do you know what that means? You said, 'Whatever this is.' I'm naming it."

He knew he sounded like a crazy man—words tumbling. He didn't care anymore. He wasn't afraid. He had to say it.

"Sam, wait..."

"I can't. I can't wait anymore, Mildred. I'm in love with you. I've fallen hopelessly, helplessly, crazy in love with you. I think you are the most amazing woman I've ever met. I can't stop thinking about you. Part of me is afraid this is too beautiful to be real. That's why I haven't minded taking it slow. Because I've loved every minute we get to spend together—even if it's only long distance. But I am ready to be with you. I want to touch you so bad some nights I can't sleep for the want of it. I replay that moment over and over in my mind—the one moment I touched you."

Mildred closed her eyes. "Me too."

"I remember how soft your skin is, the way you smell like apples, that dimple in your cheek. It's like air to me—that memory."

Mildred's breath came in soft, silent flutters.

"But I don't want to stop there, Mildred. I want more memories with you. Of—of touching you. I know this is not the ordinary way to have a relationship. Some days the weirdness of it all makes me lose my mind a little, like it's not real, like it could disappear so fast I couldn't stop it. But it *is* real, Mil. It's the only way I can have you right now and I'll take it. But it won't always be like this. I promise we'll be together for real. Very soon. Please don't give up on us before we even get started."

Suddenly, he was quiet and Mildred could hear her heart pounding in her ears.

"Mil?"

"I'm here."

"What do you think?"

What did she think? It seemed like anything she could say would not be enough.

"I don't know," she said, weakly. "I-I can't say. I mean, that word, *love,* it scares me, Sam."

Sam was quiet a minute. Then, "That's okay. You just need a little time. Soon, you'll see there's nothing to be afraid of."

"Yes, but..."

"Listen, Mil. All you need to know is, I'm going to win your trust."

"But it's not—all I need to know. I need to know you're not going to leave. I need to know you won't become a stranger to me. I need a guarantee, and I know there is none. I need to deal with that...in *me,* Sam. Please understand. I just need a little time to think this through. Please?"

Sam was tired.

"What does that mean, Mil?"

"I don't know, Sam. You'll be here for the concert in about four weeks. I promise I'll figure this out before then."

"Four weeks?"

She couldn't help smiling at his incredulity.

"I said *before* four weeks. Four weeks or so."

"Give me a date."

"What do you mean?"

"When may I see you again?"

Mildred thought. "The show is the ninth, right?"

"Yeah. The show before is in Columbus on the seventh. Then, I'm off until D.C. on the sixteenth."

"So, could you come a day early? On Thursday? The eighth?"

"We originally planned that, remember? A day early is good for setup and all, to go over logistics. I was going to stay for a week, right? Until D.C., so we could spend time together. You owe me a tour of the farm, remember?"

"I remember."

Mildred tried to find a reason to say no to the extra week but couldn't.

"Okay. The eighth it is," she said. "Could we play it by ear after that?"

"Play it by ear?" He sighed heavily. "And until the eighth, you mean no calls, no FaceTime, no nothing?"

"I think so."

Sam sighed again. "Whatever you need, Mildred. I won't call."

"Thank you."

"And, Mil?"

"Umhum?"

"I do. Love you."

Day 3

Moonflower,

I promised not to text you, or call you, or FaceTime you, but we said nothing of email, or snail mail, or carrier pigeon. It has only been three days since we spoke and I surprise myself by the many times I've said, "I can't wait to tell Mildred." So, if it's okay with you, for every day we cannot speak, I will send you a poem inspired by missing you. I'm not asking you to respond. Four weeks, "or so" has never seemed so long.

I love you.

I miss you.

—*Sam*

your absence
at my door leaves
a long shadow. I
put my hand to the
empty frame.

you are

scent of apple in
the rain
slip of leaf
light-tipping over water
snow-capped
mountain peak
rising near
    the hollows of me.

the air waits
for the echo of us
to begin again
begin again

Day 4

without you, I am
thin as the wings
of a Luna, moonlit,
translucent

your gaze
I remember

I want to touch
your skin—
lend my powdery film
to your luminous
fingers

Day 5

sleep
with me under the open sky;

let your hands be the fires
that warm me—

wild honeysuckle,
nape of your neck

dark kissing the edge
of day.

your skin like stars
our breath in the night

I am mist
of morning-to-come,
glistening over
all of you *(all of you)*

sleep with me
under
the open sky

Day 6

a thousand
unwritten poems
in my bed—
your hands, your eyes

goldenrod
blossoming light across
the hollowed out
places

my breath pale
in the night

I cannot forget
you

Day 7

the maple leaves shimmer silver
in the fading light of evening

I touch the grasses of the meadow with my mind
walk through the myth that I am separate from all this

I remember how you looked that first night
vulnerable and sweet

did your mother carry you on one hip, dream
your wedding day?

the thought of you in white lace feels like Eden,
the river forks again

I feel a bass drum echo through my ribs,
yearn for your hand in mine

the beads on the abacus of time
click softly as they meet

let's sit together
as the night begins to sing

MILDRED

[august-september]

The poems were a distraction. Every morning they came, sometimes sent at two or three a.m. After reading, she was weak with longing.

let your hands be the fires
that warm me—

For Pete's sake! How could a girl's head not be turned? But still.

It was the unspoken belief that made her hesitate. She was reluctant to admit she still carried it after fifteen years. The belief that one day Levi would return.

Mildred crept to the lower cabinets of the built-ins and opened a door. She pushed aside bins of old photographs until she found the gilded box. Pulling it from its nesting place, she carried it to the overstuffed chair. It sat on her lap for a long time, her palms resting on the lid. Then, with a deep inhalation, she lifted the top.

All that was left of her love with Levi Johnston.

On top was a photo of her in her grandmother's wedding dress—one month before they were to marry, used for the announcement in the paper. She picked up the black and white photograph.

the thought of you in white lace feels like Eden...

Mildred studied her face in the photo. She was so young, barely twenty years old. But she had loved Levi for such a long time. She placed the photo on the cushion beside her and sifted through more memories.

Their engagement pictures.

Her heart moved at the sight of him. That shock of white-blond hair, that toothy grin. All his sun-kissed goodness. How could she have known that when these pictures were taken he had already started using the poison that would change everything forever?

"We were so happy," she whispered to the photograph.

A tear fell on the photo and Mildred quickly wiped it away, wiped her eyes and her face roughly with her hands. Someone came into the room and lingered in the doorway. Mildred felt the presence, but did not look up. Then, Delal was beside her.

"Are you okay?" she signed, brow wrinkled.

Mildred tried to smile. She nodded. "Yes, I'm fine. Thank you," she signed back.

Delal sat on the ottoman in front of Mildred. She looked at the picture in Mildred's hands and gestured to it.

"Is he," she traced across Levi in the photo, "the reason S-A-M (she spelled his name out slowly) does not call?"

Mildred shook her head. "No." She pointed to herself. "I am the reason."

Delal looked puzzled. "Do you love this boy?" she gestured to Levi again.

Mildred struggled to find sign language to explain, "I used to. A long time ago," she said, as she tried to piece together the signs.

Delal nodded knowingly. A cloud crossed her face. "Hard to forget. L-O-V-E."

Mildred took Delal's right hand and pressed her thumb into her palm. Delal closed her fingers around Mildred's touch. Sorrow felt like a person, and they sat with it a moment.

"I'm sorry," Mildred signed.

Delal smiled a sad smile. "*D-E-Z-A* is gone. Will not come back. But for you, love not gone."

Mildred nodded, eyes welling. "But," she signed. "I am afraid."

"Of?" Delal signed back.

Mildred made the sign for "broken heart."

Delal nodded. "Fear. But broken heart is open. More room for love." She gestured to Mildred's heart. "Your heart, more room. For me. For girls. For this." She gestured around her, at the house, the grounds. "For *S-A-M*."

Mildred looked at Delal. This woman had lost so much. And *she* was counseling Mildred. "I don't know," she signed. "If he leaves."

Delal put a hand on Mildred's cheek, rested it there a moment. A knowing look came over her face. "You can," she signed. She kissed Mildred on both cheeks and left her with the box.

Mildred touched her cheek where Delal's hand had just been. She thought about Deza and the ache of emptiness she had felt these past few days.

Mildred took out her phone and hit "FaceTime."

SAM

[september]

Dear Moonflower,

I am the happiest man. Seeing your face yesterday was a gift. I have grown accustomed to writing you poetry every day. I think I will continue the practice.

I love you.

—*Sam*

you said
wrap yourself in light
and love will come to you

I quietly wept
moonbeam,
starlight

~

Sam threw his duffel onto the backseat and climbed in beside Renault.

"Let's hit it, man. I-64 all the way. Tonight, we sleep in style in West Virginia."

Renault smiled as he pulled his seatbelt over his shoulder. "I've never seen you like this, man. You got it bad for this girl. Never thought I'd see the day."

Sam grinned. No use denying truth.

"We are headed to the country, Renault. What do you think of that, city boy? I'll tell Mildred to give you a room with a view."

"I'm looking forward to meeting Miss Mildred. This woman needs to be warned about where she puts her affections."

Sam landed a playful punch to his friend's arm. "Don't even joke. She's been a little skittish. What I need you to do is reinforce what a stand-up kind of guy I am."

Renault rolled his eyes. "Why don't you take a nap, Sam. It's countryside all the way there."

~

Mildred held a long-stemmed red rose. She lifted the bud to her nose and breathed in, eyes closed. Then she held it out for Sam to smell. Sam breathed in the spicy fragrance, pulled her to him and covered her mouth with his...

Then: a loud string of curses from Renault. Sam opened his eyes as a sickening thunk jarred the van and an animal flew up over the hood, shattered the windshield, and disappeared. He screamed as the van careened off the side of the road and nose-dived down a small embankment, coming to a jerking stop.

"Are you all right?" The fear in Renault's voice made Sam take stock of himself. He was shaken up and his right shoulder hurt from knocking into the door. "I think so. You?"

There was a small cut on Renault's forehead. "Yeah, I'm fine.

Thank God for seatbelts."

"What the hell happened?"

"Deer."

Sam had a sinking feeling. He looked around. They were a good distance off the road, safe from oncoming traffic. He stared up the desolate highway. Not a car in sight.

They sat in stunned silence a moment and then, as if in some unspoken agreement, opened their doors simultaneously and walked around to the front of the van. Both front tires were blown. The front of the van was crumpled and, from the smell of things, the coolant tank was busted. A quiet hissing sound came from beneath the hood.

They looked up and down the quiet four-lane.

"Where are we?" Sam asked.

"Not quite to West Virginia yet. We've only been on the road about an hour. Just passed Lexington about twenty minutes ago. Somewhere around the George Washington and Jefferson National Forest."

Renault was tapping his phone. "I barely have two bars, but I see a towing service just outside of Lexington." He tapped the number. "Yeah, uh, hello. We just had an accident out here on I-64—hit a deer. Our van is undrivable." He gestured to Sam. "Get the insurance card, would you?"

Sam did as he was told. As Renault negotiated their rescue, he walked to the edge of the road to see if the poor creature who caused all this could be found. Just as he spotted the still form in the eastbound lanes, a state trooper passed by. The officer slowed down and edged around the deer's body. Then he flipped on his lights and drove up just far enough to hit an emergency turn lane. He pulled up along the berm behind the lopsided van.

The trooper climbed out of his cruiser and Sam walked up to greet him, hand extended.

"Afternoon, officer." *He looked all of twenty-five years old in his broad-rimmed hat and dark glasses.* The trooper took Sam's hand and gave it a firm shake.

"Hello, sir, Trooper Ojeda. Everyone here all right?"

"Yes, sir. We're a little shaken up but no serious injuries. Unfortunately, can't say the same about our friend over there."

They both looked at the deer in the middle of the road. "I'll call the road-crew to clean that up."

Trooper Ojeda nodded towards Renault. "Your friend getting the tow taken care of?"

"Yeah. Some place in Lexington."

Ojeda shook his head. "You just got a ten-point buck. Shame to waste it. You want a kill tag? Know anyone who could use the meat?"

"A *what* tag?" Sam tried not to look at how dead the deer was. "Oh! No, ah, we're not from around here. You know anyone who might want it?"

"We have a group of hunters 'round these parts that will do the dressing and give the meat to the food bank. You're sure you don't want it?"

"Nah. I'd be glad if they'd put it to good use."

"Much obliged. Want to keep the rack?"

Sam stared at the young man. "Oh, thanks. I'm not much of a trophy guy. But thanks for asking."

Trooper Ojeda nodded, took out his radio and started talking. "Len, can you send someone from Hogan's Heroes down here to mile marker 43 to collect a donation. Fella just got himself a ten-point buck."

~

"I can't believe we made it this far and I still won't get to see you tonight." At the garage, Sam finally had time to call Mildred. "I know, I know it could have been worse. I'm just disappointed."

Sam glanced over at Renault who, somehow, had gotten hold of a box of tissues. He plucked one out of the box and offered it to Sam. Sam glared, then got up and pushed through the door of the garage waiting room.

"Renault is renting a truck and hauling the van—wrecked as it is, Scotty wants it—back to Nashville. But as soon as we're done here, I'll rent a car and head that way."

He paced back and forth in the parking lot.

"Nah, all the equipment was on the bus, no worries."

He studied a caterpillar inching its way across a yellow line.

"Ok, Mil. I'll keep you posted." He hesitated then added, "Love you." Every time he said it, the world started to spin. She did not respond. "See you soon."

He hung up and stood still. The sky was the kind of blue you squeeze from a paint tube—saturated and cloudless. Sam rubbed his throbbing shoulder and tried to think good things. Mildred was right, he or Renault could have been seriously hurt. And Mildred would come around. He knew it. He closed his eyes and focused on gratitude.

~

"500C? What does the C stand for?"

"Cabrio." The girl behind the counter looked twelve years old. How could she possibly rent him a car? "It's kind of a convertible thing. I love it. Only thing is, it's this weird lime color. Some kind of special edition. That's how dad got it. Nobody else at auction wanted it." She chomped on a wad of gum with her mouth open.

"Dad?"

"Yeah, my dad owns this place."

"Ah." That explained it. "Well, don't you have something more...more..."

"Masculine?" she smiled.

Sam shrugged sheepishly. "I guess so."

"Maybe? It's the Fiat or a 1979 Corvette. And between you and me, the Corvette's not very reliable. Broke down on a guy just last week. But I think he felt very manly until we had to send a minivan to pick him up on the side of the road. I figure, the Fiat gets better gas mileage. Weather's nice. You can put the top down."

Sam sighed. "Let me see if my guitar will fit in the Fiat."

Renault stayed with the van, so he could accompany it back to Nashville. Sam didn't get on the road until just after four p.m.

I should be there in three hours. Save a dinner plate for me, he texted Mildred.

Which would have been true if not for the interstate. At five-thirty, just outside of Lewisburg, West Virginia, the road became a parking lot. It was backed up as far as he could see. He texted Mildred. *Is there some kind of construction on 64 around Lewisburg? Traffic at a dead stop here.*

He waited. Didn't move more than a car length in twenty minutes. Mildred rang in on his phone.

"Hey, Mil. What's up?"

"Oh, Sam. You're not going to believe this."

"Try me."

"There's an accident near Lewisburg. Multiple vehicles. Tractor trailer caught on fire. The interstate is closed in both directions."

"Of course it is."

"They're detouring everyone over route 60. If the traffic is moving okay, it should take just three more hours."

"The traffic is not moving okay."

The other end of the line was silent. Sam sighed.

"Where do I get on this route 60?"

"Right at Lewisburg. There should be signs or officers directing traffic that way." She paused. "I'm sorry, sweet."

He sighed again. "It's okay. I'll see you tonight. As soon as all the forces in the universe allow."

"Oh, now. It's not so bad. You'll be here before you know it. By the way, the guys are here. We parked the bus in the big barn for the stay. They've already unloaded the equipment. So you're off the hook for that." He could feel her smile.

Sam looked at the new route he called up on his phone. Three hours. If he got moving soon.

"That's good. Tell them I should be there tonight sometime."

~

Four hours later he was in Montgomery, West Virginia and the traffic was starting to break free. His GPS told him he was 27 miles from Malden, the small town outside of Charleston where The Gardens was situated. *It's a good thing,* he thought. *Barely one bar on the signal.*

And he really had to pee.

They called this portion of route 60 The Midland Trail, Mildred had told him when she checked in about a half hour ago. It was a scenic highway that passed through some of the most beautiful parts of the sate. "You should get off at Fayetteville," she told him, "and see the New River Gorge Bridge. It's the third highest bridge in the United States and it's such a view."

"Mildred," he'd said, "it's going to be dark soon. Besides, the only view I want to see right now is your face. And the rest of you."

Her nervous laughter gave him butterflies and, remembering now, he caught a bit of the flying sensation she gave him. "Calm down, Sam," he said aloud. "You aren't there yet. Keep your head in the game."

It *was* beautiful countryside. Weathered barns and ancient farmhouses. Sloping, tree-blanketed mountains hugging the river. Sam wished he had more time to enjoy the drive. But The Midland Trail and everything along it was fast swallowed up by darkness. His bladder gave a cry of discomfort. Yeah, scenic, but not much for gas stations or rest areas. He would cut up one of the narrow off-roads he kept passing and find a tree.

He turned down the next country road. "Make the nearest U-turn," his GPS said. "Ah, shut up," he muttered as he bumped along the narrow road. It seemed even darker, the trees blocking any remaining light from the sky. He leaned into the windshield and squinted. The further in he went, the more it looked like a cow path. This was going nowhere. "Screw it." Sam stopped the car in the middle of the path, dimmed the lights to parking, and hopped out to relieve himself.

"Make the nearest U-turn," the voice called after him.

After he did his business, Sam thanked the tree and stumbled down a small embankment to return to the car. At the last, he lost his footing and fell softly onto his hands and knees right into the middle of the path. The ground was soft from recent rains and the grass was cool and springy under his hands. Earth-scent bid him roll over onto his back and stare up at the sky. The waning crescent moon was suspended like a smile. The Big Dipper tipped low, pouring starlight over everything. He shivered under the cool of late summer, and suddenly became aware of cricket-song filling the air. He tried to count the number of chirps per fourteen seconds to guestimate the temperature, remembering Dolbear's Law from biology class, but his ears weren't keen enough. He'd never seen stars burn the sky so bright and he felt his breathing slow, his muscles relax.

He didn't realize how tense he was, and this little interlude was just what he needed. He felt like he could sleep all night under the music of the stars. If only Mildred was with him. At that thought, he hopped up, went back to the car, and turned the lights on bright to see if there was a convenient turn around up ahead. He couldn't make out much by way of the road so he drove on a little ways to see what he could find.

"Make the nearest U-turn."

"I thought I told you to shut it." Sam drove on up the cow path. Soon, he realized if he was going to turn around he would have to make his *own* path. The ground on the right was level with the road, but overgrown with grass and shrubs. He would have to find the least overgrown spot.

"Recalculating."

Oh! Well, maybe this little road did come out somewhere.

"Proceed 1.2 miles to Midland Trail."

It must circle back around. He glanced at the odometer to measure 1.2 miles. He wished the little Fiat was all-wheel drive. He crept along in the dark, barely able to see up ahead. The road seemed to get narrower and narrower. After twenty minutes, Sam picked up his phone to see if the map would be useful.

"What the...?" The screen refreshed under his thumb and the map disappeared from the screen. No service.

Suddenly, the right side of the Fiat sunk with a jolt. He was in some kind of ditch. "Dammit." He punched gently on the gas but the little tires just spun. He wasn't going anywhere.

Sam turned off the engine but left the lights on. He got out to see what he could see. He walked around to the passenger side, using the flashlight on his phone to light the way. The tire was stuck in a deep rut. He thought of all the movies he'd seen where the hero stacks rocks or wood under the tire to give traction, then moved the flashlight over the nearby woods and looked around for anything.

It was just too damn dark. He walked over to the embankment, scanned the woodsy area with the light and felt around for any fallen tree limbs or loose stones. Nothing. Sam looked up at the immenseness of the starry sky above him.

"He should have been here at 10:00, Russ. It is now," she looked at her watch, "11:20."

"Don't worry, Mildred. We're gonna find your guy. When did you say you last spoke with him?" Petey sniffed the leg of the officer's uniform.

"Around 9 p.m. He was about 15 miles from Montgomery. But with the traffic moving as slow as it was, it's impossible to tell where he would be at any certain time. There's no cell signal on certain parts of that route. Oh why, oh why didn't I drive out to meet him? It's not that far from here."

She put her hand to her mouth and walked to the window. Sher followed Mildred and put her arm around her. The deputy made notes.

"Don't worry, Mildred," he said again. "He probably just got tired and decided to pull over to rest. Maybe fell asleep and is oblivious."

"That's right, hon," Cindy said from the couch where she sat wedged in with Brit, Dan and Rob. "He probably just fell asleep."

Mildred looked out the window into the dark night. "I don't know," she said absently. "It's just not like him. The show is at noon. He would want to be here tonight to make sure everything is ready. It's not like him to just let that go."

Deputy Russ looked at a stack of concert flyers sitting on

the coffee table. "Do you mind if I take one of these? Might be helpful to have a picture of Sam."

"Of course!" Mildred picked up one of the posters to hand to Russ. She looked at Sam's face smiling up at her and a small whimper rose in her throat.

~

"Have you found anything?"

Everyone had fallen asleep spread around the sunroom, and when Mildred's cell phone rang at 7 a.m., every eye had blinked open.

"Well, yes and no."

"What do you mean?"

"We found the car. All his stuff: cell phone, guitar, duffel. But Sam was gone."

"What?"

"Yeah, found a lime green Fiat up a trail just outside of Montgomery. The front passenger wheel was stuck in a pretty deep ditch. From the looks of things, he tried to get it out but just ground in deeper."

Mildred's mind was racing.

"Well, then, he must have tried to walk somewhere? Were there tracks or notes or anything?"

"There were footprints everywhere. No notes. And some ATV tracks. From the looks of things, they tried to pull the vehicle out of the ditch.."

"So, you think Sam went off with this ATV rider?"

"If he was still there when they came upon the vehicle. He may have tried to walk somewhere and maybe they saw this abandoned Fiat and thought they'd take it for a ride. I just don't know why he wouldn't have taken his cell phone, at least. The keys were still in the ignition."

This last bit gave Mildred pause. There were all kinds of characters in these hills.

~

She headed out over the back porch into the disappearing night. Petey followed, his nose gently touching the backs of her legs.

Mildred needed to breathe.

Half a mile up the Hill Path, her crew had placed a couple of hammocks in a clearing. When she arrived, she sank into one, draping her legs over the edge. The blue light of night lingered, but at the edge of the sky dome, a rosy bloom flowed upward. She searched for the autumn star, Fomalhaut—or "the Lonely One" as the ancients liked to call it. It was the only bright star in the southern sky this time of year.

Robins were singing their sweet-sad morning song and she could smell a hint of smoke.

"Oh, Sam. Where are you?" she whispered.

SAM

[september]

He walked back the way he came for what felt like a couple miles, phone stretched out in front of him. Surely there was some kind of reception somewhere along this mountain! If he walked to the main road, maybe he could flag down a ride. Bleakly, he thought of the windy mountain road from which he'd strayed. Would there be any traffic at all now? Perhaps the detour was still in effect. He quickened his pace.

Night in West Virginia seemed darker than any other. This cow path trailed on endlessly. The quiet of the surrounding forest was thick, like a blanket wrapped around him, except...What was that noise? Sam slowed to a cautious creeping. A rustling just ahead, accompanied by a strange sort of low rumbly sound...not quite a growl, but...

Sam cast his phone light onto the path. It fell on a large, round eye attached to...Bear!

He turned and ran as fast as he could until he reached the stranded little Fiat. Quickly, he ducked inside and locked the doors. He hunched down and waited, heart pounding. After a few minutes of silence, he began to feel foolish. A bear! The poor creature. He probably scared it more than it scared him. He laughed out loud at himself.

"Oh, Sam. If only Mildred could only see you now."

Sam turned the ignition, then hit the button to open the top of the car. He leaned the seat back and stared up at the night sky. Mildred knew all the names of the stars. She came alive when she spoke their names. She was connected to the earth in ways he was only beginning to understand, his moonflower. He hated scaring her like this. How could he have been so stupid to not foresee a loss of service? He worried over and over until his eyes grew heavy.

The last thing he did before falling asleep was put the top up. Just in case.

~

It sounded like a chainsaw running in his head. Sam opened his eyes. Dark still filled the air, but light striated the edge of the horizon. What was that noise? He glanced at his watch: 6:07 a.m. He started as someone tapped on his window. A hairy face peered in at him. Sam turned the ignition key so he could roll down the window.

"Morning," said a gruff voice from somewhere under a huge beard. "You know you're on private property?"

Sam rubbed sleep out of his eyes. "To be honest, sir, I don't know *where* I am. I ran into a little trouble last night when I pulled off to take a leak. I was en route from Charlottesville, on my way to visit a friend in Malden. Got stuck in a ditch and couldn't get her out. No cell phone service here. I tried walking back to the main road, but I ran into a bear and..."

Steel blue eyes stared at him from under pale brows.

"A bear?"

"Yeah. A bear."

Sam looked out the windshield. He saw a large ATV with

some kind of trailer attached. He felt a momentary panic. Maybe he shouldn't have told this guy he had no cell service.

The man continued to stare at Sam. Then he turned to the side and spit tobacco juice in an arching stream.

Impressive, thought Sam.

"Let's see what we can do to get you outa here."

The man walked around to the front of the Fiat. Sam opened his door and followed.

Thin under his insulated coveralls, but broad-shouldered, wiry muscles rippled under cloth and Sam swallowed hard as he noted the rifle casually slung over his shoulder. The beard gave the appearance he was older than he really was. What Sam had initially mistaken for the white hair of age, he could better see now was flaxen blond. This guy was probably even younger than him. They stopped in front of the Fiat. Sam's companion put his hands on his hips and studied the car. "You got her stuck real good, didn't ya?"

"Yeah. It was dark and I couldn't tell what I was up against. Sam Gillenwater is the name." He stuck out his hand. The other man hesitated a minute before taking it.

"You can call me Johnston," he said, before turning away. "That's all you need to know about me. Johnstons have been on this mountain for over two hundred years. Only one other family been here longer. That's the Ruffners on the other side of the mountain."

"Funny you should say that, Mr. Johnston. That's where I was headed—to Mildred Ruffner's place. I'm a musician and I'm scheduled to do a concert at her bed and breakfast at noon today. It's a fundraiser. That's where I was headed when I got hung up."

At the mention of Mildred's name, Johnston's head snapped

up. He studied Sam in silence. When he finally spoke, his voice was soft. "Are you a friend of Mildred's?"

The hair on the back of Sam's neck prickled and he was suddenly *very* aware of the gun slung over Johnston's shoulder.

"Yeah. You might say that. And she must be worried sick about me. She was expecting me last night around ten."

Johnston's blue eyes seemed to flash as he continued to study Sam intently. A silence hung between them. Then, suddenly, he looked away from Sam into the brushy meadow. "Well, then, we'd better get you out of here as fast as we can. Can't have Mildred worrying."

~

They tried everything. The trouble was, the ground was too wet and the tires stubbornly dug in deeper. After about half an hour Johnston decided Sam was giving too much gas so they traded places. Sam pushed from behind as Johnston gently applied pressure to the gas.

It happened so fast Sam could do nothing to stop it. As the Fiat rocked to-and-fro, trying to break free from the ditch, he lost his footing. He slipped off the path and fell into the brush, swiping his left arm roughly on a sharp tree stump sticking up. It hurt like hell. Sam pulled up his sleeve to look at the damage, and saw a huge gash down his right forearm, blood gushing from the wound.

"Hold on!" he shouted. Johnston cut the engine.

At the sight of the blood, Sam started to get woozy. Then everything went black.

~

When he came to, Sam found himself alone in a low-ceilinged room with clapboard walls. He tried to move but his arms and legs were restrained. He remembered Johnston. The gun slung over his shoulder. Sam felt a rush of panic and started flailing about, pulling against the bindings on his limbs. A sharp pain shot through his left forearm.

"Ho, ho, ho, ho!" Someone rushed through the door. "You're going to undo all the good work I've done on your arm."

Johnston's bearded face appeared above him, his blue eyes boring into Sam's before turning on the arm. He put his hands on Sam's shoulders and gently pushed him down onto the mattress. "Settle down." Once again those eyes pierced Sam's. "Sorry for this. I was trying to stitch you up and couldn't take the chance you'd come to and sock me a good one." Sam stilled under the firm pressure of Johnston's weight. "I'll loose you in a minute. But first, I want to ask you a few questions." He released Sam of his weight and walked to the window.

"Stitch me up? Where the hell are we?" Sam was trying to make sense of it all. He looked at his arm and saw it was neatly wrapped in white gauze. He leaned back against the pillow, head spinning.

"This is my family's hunting camp. My brothers and I used to come up here every year this time—get ready for bow season at the end of the month. But this is my first time back in fifteen years."

Fifteen years ago I was to marry. Sam frowned. He felt uneasy.

Johnston studied him. "Calm down. You're safe here. I'll get you over to Mildred as soon as I can. You gave me quite the scare there, brother. I thought you hit your head."

Sam shook his head. "I've got a thing about blood. Makes

me pass out every time."

"Lucky for you I've got some medic training. It's not the first time I've had to stitch someone up out here in the wilderness."

"I'd feel luckier if you'd untie me."

Johnston continued to study Sam from under bushy brows.

"All in good time," he said, turning his back to Sam. "I want to know about Mildred." He faced Sam now. "How is she?"

Sam looked him in the eye. *Is this what a raving lunatic looks like?* He pondered Johnston's sharp gaze and steady hands. He seemed as sane as anyone.

"Mildred is very well. She's doing what she loves to do. She's happy."

Johnston's eyes were blue fire. "And you? What about you, Sam Gillenwater? What are you to Mildred?"

Sam swallowed but did not lower his eyes.

"I am in love with her."

"And does Mildred love you too?"

"Well, that's a good question. I believe she does, though she hasn't said so. It's been a little tricky. If you know Mildred, then you might know," he maintained his gaze, "she was hurt pretty bad by someone a long time ago."

Johnston's face twisted into a grisly smile and again he turned his back to Sam. Then, in one fluid movement Sam could only describe as graceful, he dipped, scooped the gun up in his arms and pointed it in Sam's face. There was a tiny film of sweat on his brow, despite the chill in the room.

"Do you think you know something about that?" he snarled, his left eye staring down the sight on the rifle.

Sam's father's kind face was before him. *Do you hear that, Sammy?* He did. He listened to his heart beat in his ears, could feel blood pumping through his veins. Sam held Johnston's gaze. "I only know what Mildred's told me," he said, softly, as if speaking too loudly might cause the gun to go off.

Johnston looked aside but kept the gun aimed in Sam's direction for a few more claustrophobic seconds before letting the butte fall, point to the floor. He walked back to the window, dangling the rifle at his side, then lifted the blind, and the sun glared in on them both. Sam blinked, his heart took off racing— as if it was the first time it had ever pumped blood. Outside, a forest was donning autumn's reds and yellows, green still mingled in. Johnston leaned his forehead on the window. "I've made a lot of mistakes in my life. But the one I regret most is hurting Mildred." He gently leaned the gun up against the window casing and turned to face Sam.

"She deserves to be happy. Will you promise me? That she'll be happy with you?" His eyes were moist and he opened his mouth to say more but suddenly the door flew open and they were no longer alone. Several other men began filing into the small room, all armed. A burlier, bushier-bearded version of Johnston stepped out of the rush of men and, with a grace that surprised Sam, was at the window and had Johnston's rifle in his hands before anyone could stop him.

"Brother," the man said to Johnston, "we've only just gotten you back. Are you so eager to be taken from us again?"

Johnston blinked, a confused expression on his face. "Cody? What are you and the boys doing here?"

A tall man with a gleaming bald head moved over to Sam and began untying his restraints.

"Now, that's a good question, Levi." said the man called Cody. "Me and the boys were out at the other camp—hauling some wood, cleaning up—you know, the usual, when a deputy stopped by. Wanted to know if we'd seen a stranger around, a man who's been missing for several hours. 'Course we had no information for him, but we told him we'd keep our eye out. When we heard this missing fellow was a friend of Mildred's, we thought we'd better check up on you. Imagine our distress when you were not where we left you. Left you with strict instructions to stay put."

"I-I needed to get outside. I was going stir-crazy all cooped up like that." Johnston's voice trailed off and he lifted both hands to rub his eyes.

Cody continued. "And Hope said you didn't take your medication this morning."

"I don't like how it makes me feel, Cody. Like I'm trapped inside myself..."

Cody let out a frustrated breath. He put both hands on Johnston's shoulders and turned him around so they were face-to-face.

"Levi. Look at me."

Johnston lifted his eyes to his brother's face. Cody leaned in.

"You've got to take your medication." Johnston started to object but Cody talked over him. "You've GOT to take it, little brother. Maybe not forever, but for right now, you've got to. We've got to get you well, Levi." He lifted the rifle with his right hand. "And you know firearms are off limits for now. What if that deputy had found you instead of us? And here you are, with the missing stranger all tied up. They would have taken you straight to the county jail. We can't lose you again." His voice broke. "Do you know how much trouble you're in, Levi? I can't fix this one, brother. Kidnapping is a serious charge..."

"He didn't kidnap me."

Sam sat up on the edge of the bed, rubbed his wrists where the bindings had been.

Cody looked from Levi to Sam. "Excuse me?"

"He didn't kidnap me. He was trying to help me. I got my car hung up and while we were trying to get it out of the mud, I fell and hurt my arm. Levi stitched me up. We were just talking about getting me over to Mildred's place when you all arrived."

Cody studied Sam's face. "Trying to help you? Then, mister, why were you tied to that bed just now?"

Sam shrugged. "Precautionary measure."

"Precautionary measure?" Cody continued to stare into Sam's eyes. A muscle twitched in his jaw. "Mister, you better get your story straight. I don't know what has happened here this morning, but I do know this doesn't look good. And my brother could go to jail."

Sam shook his head. He locked eyes with Levi. "No one here is going to jail. Levi was helping me. I'll be glad to tell the deputy the whole story."

Levi dropped his gaze. "I'm sorry, Sam. I'm sorry if I scared you. I didn't mean…"

Sam, uncertain what to do, stood up. "It's okay, Levi. I think I understand a little better about things now." He stuck out his hand. Levi looked into Sam's face before gripping the outstretched hand.

"Thank you, Sam." He looked into Sam's eyes. "I can see you are a good man. That makes me glad."

The other men moved in to surround them. "Why don't you introduce me to this mob?" Sam said.

Levi only hesitated a second, then grinned. "This is my family."

He nodded in the direction of the bald guy who had freed Sam's bindings. "This knob of a man is my brother-in-law, Ford."

"Howdy," Ford said.

Sam nodded. "Nice to meet you, Ford. Thanks for freeing me up there a minute ago."

"No worries," Ford said. "Never know what I'll be called to do when keeping company with these knuckleheads." He grinned.

"These other ugly mugs are my brothers," said Levi. "That's Jonah," he pointed with his thumb to a skinny, clean-faced kid in a ball cap who nodded at Sam. "Micah," a somewhat stockier version of Jonah nodded also. "Jeremiah," a slightly smaller version of Levi with a tamer beard. "and Amos, Jeremiah's twin." The twin nodded, and Sam was glad to see he was clean-shaven. Otherwise, he may have never kept them straight. "And our senior sibling, Cody." Levi nodded to the burly figure beside Amos.

Sam thought Cody grinned under his beard. "Our ma didn't find the Lord til after I was born." He guffawed and the others chuckled. Sam laughed too.

"Fellas, this here is Sam Gillenwater," Levi said.

"Sam Gillenwater?" Jonah stepped forward and peered at Sam's face in the dim light of approaching morning. "Well. It *is* you." He took off his ball cap and offered his hand. "I'm a big fan of your music."

Sam took his hand. "Thanks, Jonah. I'm supposed to be giving a concert near here at noon today. If you guys can get me where I need to be, and you want 'em, I'll make sure you all have tickets."

The others moved forward. "Yeah, I know you," said Amos. "You got that 'Oddbird' song on the radio, right?"

"That's me," Sam smiled.

"I really like that song," Cody said.

"Thanks, man."

Cody spit a stream of tobacco juice into a cup he was holding. "So. You got detained by a ditch last night."

"Yeah, you could say that."

"Boy, you just ain't having any kind of luck."

"No, I am not."

"If you's supposed to give a concert at noon, we'd better get you moving. It's 11:00 right now."

"Eleven! Say, does there happen to be cell phone service here?"

Jonah spoke up. "It's weak but it usually works. Depends on your carrier."

Sam felt in his pocket for his phone. "Shoot! I must have left my phone in the car. Could I borrow one of you all's to call Mildred real fast? She must be beside herself."

"You need to call—ah—Mildred?" Cody took off his ball cap and looked sideways at Levi.

"Yeah, didn't the deputy tell you? The concert is at her bed and breakfast. That's where I was headed when I got hung up."

Cody rocked back on his heels, hat in hands. "Mildred Ruffner is one of the finest human beings you could ever meet."

Sam looked from brother to brother.

"Yes. She sure is. She must be worried sick about me. As I told your brother here," he nodded to Levi, "she was expecting me last night."

Cody tossed him his cell phone. "Give mine a try." He turned to Jonah. "Boy, go back down the hill and get Sam's things out of the car. I'm guessing he'll be wanting his phone. And his guitar."

Sam made the call, and when he hung up, the room was silent. "I'll wait for you outside," Cody said and left the room. The other brothers filed out, one-by-one, until he was left alone with Levi.

Levi sat in the chair beside the window. He put his elbows on his knees and studied the floor. "I don't know what to say, Sam. Thank you. I'm not quite myself these days."

Sam walked over and put his hand on Levi's shoulder. "I don't know what kind of hell you've been through, Levi. Take care of yourself. Get well. I think the person Mildred loved all those years ago is still in you."

~

The shortcut over the mountain turned out to be an old, over-grown path. Cody tossed him a helmet. "It's a rough ride. This path probably hasn't been used much for fifteen years."

He grew up over the mountain from me.

Sam glanced at his watch one more time before they took off to a jerking start. The rumble of the engine quieted any questions he could ask. Out loud anyway. But inside he was feeling all kinds of conflicted. Thinking about Mildred loving someone the way she described her first love. Levi. *He had all my loves...*

He shook his head to dust loose these thoughts. He'd have to wait for Mildred to tell her story. She was the only one he wanted to hear it from. Now, he was enjoying the wildness of Ruffner Mountain.

Ten minutes later, scratched and burr-riddled, Cody and Sam roared into The Gardens. It was almost noon and the sun had just started to rise over the meadow. Cody rumbled the ATV to a stop right outside what Sam knew must be the kitchen door. It flew open immediately.

Cody took off his helmet.

"Hello there, Cindy. I believe I found someone you've been looking for."

Sam climbed off the back, removed his helmet, and began unstrapping his guitar from the rack. Cindy dried her hands on a towel.

She yelled behind her, "He's here! He's safe!"

She looked at the man standing beside Sam and slowly walked to him. "Cody Johnston? Is that you under all that facial hair?"

Cody returned Cindy's gaze. "It is."

Cindy was quiet a moment.

"What in the world have you been up to? How did you find Sam? How are you?"

Cody laughed. "One question at a time, woman!" He coughed and looked at Sam. "I suspect we'll have time to catch up in the near future. For now, I think you'd better get Sam here where he needs to be to start this concert he's told me about."

Cindy started. "Yes! That's right." She hurried over to Sam and took the guitar out of his hands. "You probably need to clean up a bit. Let me show you where to go." Cindy poked her head back through the door. "Delal! Delal, come here!"

A beautiful woman appeared in the doorframe behind Cindy. When she saw Sam, her eyes widened. "Go tell the others," Cindy said. "Then run up to the amphitheater and tell Mil Sam is on his way." Delal disappeared.

Cody shifted in his seat and lifted the helmet. "Wait!" Sam reached out and touched his arm. He stilled. "The concert. Jonah said he'd like to come. Will you all be our guests? I don't know how I can ever thank you."

"I don't think it's a good idea, Sam." Cody pulled the helmet over his head. "The best way you can thank us is to make our Mildred smile." He started the engine and took off back up the mountain. Cindy and Sam stood and watched him disappear into a frock of white pines.

Then Sam was swarmed. Sher was first, laughing and crying at the same time. "Oh, brother. You are in so much trouble." She wrapped her arms around his midsection and buried her face in his chest.

"Where are the girls?"

"I sent them with Frank up to the show already. I didn't want them to see us fretting."

Next, the guys descended upon him, patting his back and talking at once. Brit gave him a bear hug, lifting him off the ground. "You gave us a scare."

"*I* gave *me* a scare. Shouldn't you guys be up at the stage? Warming up?"

"Everything's all set and waiting for us. The Mountain Band is opening, then Ristach's going to do a short set—Mildred figured that'd give you time to get here and get ready. You've got a little time to shower if you need to—quickly! We wanted to be here when you arrived, but we're going to head on up and make sure everything's a go." They all moved out the door and Sam followed a short ways but did not continue up Stone Path with the others. "Where's Mil, Cindy?" He scanned the horizon as he moved around the house.

Cindy followed Sam. "She's up at the amphitheater. She wanted to wait for you down here but there were too many details that kept popping up. I sent Delal to let her know you've made it."

Sam could hear the steady beat of a bass drum in the distance. They reached the back porch. There sat Wren and Dí Kay, drinking hot tea, the older woman tethered to an oxygen tank. Kay looked thin enough to disappear any minute. Sam nearly tripped over the steps getting to her.

"Dí Kay! No one told me you were here!"

She smiled sweetly. "It was a surprise."

Sam hugged her gently. "I want to hear how you're doing. But right now, I need to get ready for the show."

Kay nodded. "Of course."

Cindy hooked her arm through Sam's. "This way, sir."

DELAL

[september 9]

There were so many people.

And the music was so loud.

Delal stretched her neck and searched for Mildred's pearl face and ebony hair. She would be near the stage, would she not? She edged past a couple who were standing in the grass, leaning into each other and swaying to the music. Everyone was standing. She couldn't see over their bodies. She squeezed through the crowd, setting her sights on the stage. But the closer she drew, the more people there were People on blankets. People dancing, laughing, sitting in lawn chairs in sunglasses, talking loudly, singing along.

Delal's head hurt. *Are all such music shows so noisy? Why do they not give their attention to the performers? Be quiet and listen?* She was feeling annoyed when a young man tripped and spilled a glass of wine down the front of her kitchen apron.

"I'm so sorry!" he said, before dabbing at her with a napkin. She waved him off, a wild look in her eyes, and pushed deeper into the crowd. *There!* She saw Mildred talking to a bearded man in blue jean overalls and a sports jacket. Delal set her jaw and wove to the front of the crowd. Just as she was about to break through, a man grabbed her arm.

"Hey! You can't go up there. We were here first. If you wanted the first row you should have come early. Put in your time waiting."

Delal tried to pull free but he had a firm grip on her upper arm. She shoved him away but this only made him clutch harder. "I'm serious, lady. Go find another spot."

Delal felt her face turning red. Panic rose and made everything a blur. She looked at him wide-eyed.

"Let me go! Let me go, or I scream!"

"Delal?"

The man dropped Delal's arm. She turned at the sound of her name.

"Mildred! I was trying and trying..." Her voice trailed off as she realized. She lifted her hand to her mouth and laughed out loud.

"Oh, Delal!" Mildred threw her arms around her friend. "Your voice!" Mildred put her hands on Delal's shoulders and looked her in the eye. "Is it true? Did you find your voice? Say something?"

"Sam is here!"

"Sam is here? Yes, I know, Cindy texted me. Wait? You mean Sam is up here? Delal?"

"Not up here," Delal gestured to the ground in front of her. "But Miss Cin-dee says to wait. Right here."

Mildred's eyes filled with tears. "If you and your voice stay with me, I will."

MILDRED & SAM

[september 9, noon]

Cindy took him to the wrong side of the stage. They'd meandered through the woods, "to avoid the fans," she'd said. Now, Ristach Swell was singing the last song of her set and Sam could see Mildred on the other side of all that music—so close, but so far away.

His phone buzzed.

Mildred: I see you.

Sam grinned. He looked over the piano and waved. She waved back.

Sam: I need to touch you.

Mildred: In good time. I get to introduce you. Right. Now.

He looked up to see the band leaving the stage and Mildred approaching the center mic, Petey close by her side.

"Ladies and gentlemen, give it up again for Ristach Swell and The Mountain Band!" The crowd went wild. Sam started toward Mildred, but Cindy pulled him back.

"You can't go out there yet! She has to introduce you!"

"Cindy. I see someone I want to wrap my arms around. Please do not delay me."

"I'm afraid I must." Cindy tugged on his guitar.

The crowd settled and Mildred spoke again. "Friends, we can't thank you enough for coming out today to support such a good cause. When Sam Gillenwater contacted me with the idea for The Refugee Tour, I'll admit, I was skeptical. I mean, why would a Nashville music star care about a little project we started here in West Virginia?" She glanced over at Sam in the side wing. "But I quickly learned that's the kind of man he is. A man who has the biggest heart for those who are hurting. The biggest heart of anyone I know. The way this man loves...well, it's a beautiful thing..."

Sam slipped out of his guitar strap, leaving Cindy sheepishly holding the guitar. He walked slowly toward Mildred. The crowd didn't see him at first.

Mildred continued. "And that's why—well, *one* of the reasons why..." she looked over at Sam, quickly closing the space between them. "Why I love you, Sam Gillenwater."

He closed the gap between them and swept her into his arms. When his lips touched hers, she was flying with him—soaring through blue sky. Mildred buried her face in his chest and said, "Oh, Sam!" She was crying. Happy crying.

He held her close, trembling. He breathed in her apple scent. A thousand gold balloons of love lifting into the sky.

He felt love all around them. Petey jumped up to nudge his hand. He heard the breeze kiss the grasses in the meadow. The sun shed a rosy hue at the edge of the world. The sky was music and light.

He held his Moonflower in his arms. And he felt the earth firm beneath his feet. Here. In Mildred's garden.

Also From T. S. Poetry Press

How to Read a Poem: Based on the Billy Collins Poem "Introduction to Poetry," by Tania Runyan

No reader, experienced or new to reading poems, will want to miss this winsome and surprising way into the rich, wonderful conversations that poetry makes possible.

—David Wright, Assistant Professor of English at Monmouth College, IL

The Joy of Poetry: How to Keep, Save & Make Your Life With Poems, by Megan Willome

This book is many things. An unpretentious, funny, and poignant memoir; a defense of poetry; and a response to literature that has touched her life. It's also the story of a daughter who loses her mother to cancer. The author links these things into a narrative much like that of a novel. I loved this book. As soon as I finished, I began reading it again.

—David Lee Garrison, author of *Playing Bach in the D. C. Metro*

Made in the USA
Coppell, TX
14 September 2021